THE VICTORY GARDEN

OTHER DELL YEARLING BOOKS YOU WILL ENJOY

A NECKLACE OF RAINDROPS, *Joan Aiken*

MELANIE MARTIN GOES DUTCH, *Carol Weston*

A MOTHER TO EMBARRASS ME, *Carol Lynch Williams*

TYLER ON PRIME TIME, *Steve Atinsky*

HALFWAY TO THE SKY, *Kimberly Brubaker Bradley*

ALL THE WAY HOME, *Patricia Reilly Giff*

GROVER G. GRAHAM AND ME, *Mary Quattlebaum*

SOME KIND OF PRIDE, *Maria Testa*

PURE DEAD WICKED, *Debi Gliori*

TRIA AND THE GREAT STAR RESCUE, *Rebecca Kraft Rector*

The
VICTORY GARDEN

LEE KOCHENDERFER

A Dell Yearling Book

Published by
Dell Yearling
an imprint of
Random House Children's Books
a division of Random House, Inc.
New York

The town of Shady Grove and the names of characters in this book, except those characters known to history, are fictitious.

Visit us on the Web! www.randomhouse.com/kids
Educators and librarians, for a variety of teaching tools, visit us at www.randomhouse.com/teachers

ISBN: 0-440-41703-1

Reprinted by arrangement with Delacorte Press

Printed in the United States of America

July 2003

10 9 8 7 6 5

OPM

For Harold, Kay, Julie, Harold III and Caleb

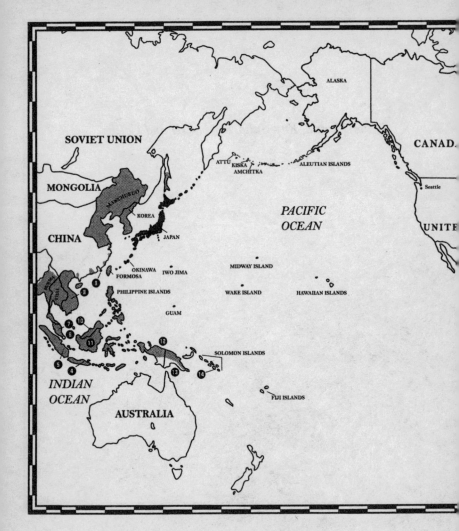

WORLD WAR II

1943

■ AXIS-OCCUPIED TERRITORIES

THE AXIS POWERS ■ Germany ■ Italy ■ Japan

(International boundaries are those that existed before the outbreak of war)

❶	Sicily	❽	French Indochina
❷	Ploesti	❾	Hong Kong
❸	Stalingrad	❿	Sarawak
❹	Java	⓫	Borneo
❺	Sumatra	⓬	New Guinea
❻	Singapore	⓭	Papua
❼	Malaya	⓮	Guadalcanal

CHAPTER 1

$\mathcal{I}$f my brother Jeff loved anything as much as he loved airplanes, which I doubt, it was tomatoes. He used to swipe them from the Burts when he went over to cut their grass, and he'd eat them right there, fresh off the vine. It's a good thing old man Burt didn't catch him, that's all I can say.

Jeff was on my mind as Dad and I worked in the garden on Saturday morning, that morning that should have been the beginning of a normal weekend. Our tomato plants were already a foot high, and it was only late April.

I tugged on the bill of my baseball cap and scanned the garden. "All clear," I said.

"Secret weapons!" said Dad.

We leaned over the plants, pulled something from our overall pockets and worked our way down the row.

"This is war!" I said.

Dad answered, "Fire away!"

I wrinkled my nose at the smell of the leaves, musty, like wet dust. The yellow blossoms smelled awful, too, but I didn't care. I was tasting the sweetness of the tomatoes to come and smelling the success of beating old man Burt again.

A movement caught my attention. I snatched the cap from my head and covered my hand with it. "Enemy approaching!" I said.

"Secure ammunition!" Dad said, shoving something into a pocket.

Behind us Tom Burt's voice bellowed. "How's that garden, Alan Marks?"

We shot up.

"Fine, Tom Burt." For some reason, the two men always called each other by their full names.

"Well, I hope you remember everything I taught you." The retired farmer was still shouting as he lumbered down a garden row, his huge frame casting a shadow over the tomatoes. Old Wolf, his German shepherd, tagged after him, tail wagging.

Burt reached down and pressed a stem between a fat thumb and finger. "You should pinch," he said to Dad. As usual, he said nothing to me. He pulled a piece off a tomato plant and dropped it to the ground.

"Hey!" I yelled. "What are you doing?"

Dad answered. "Pinching. You know. Removing

some of the leaf and blossom clusters, see?" He pulled one off and held it out to me.

"But why?" I touched the cluster. It *still* seemed wrong to throw away parts of the plants we had worked so hard to raise.

"To get better tomatoes instead of just more plant." Dad nodded toward Burt. "He taught us that one year. Made a big difference."

"But I thought—" I began, then stopped. I had caught Dad's wink.

"I shouldn't have taught you so much, Alan Marks," Mr. Burt said as he stood up. "Darned if your tomatoes weren't almost as good as mine."

"Almost?" My outburst was rude, but Tom Burt scarcely knew I was there.

"Well, the women did the deciding," he said, not to me, but to Dad. "Women don't much understand farming."

I seethed but held my tongue. I knew Dad enjoyed going at it with the old man. My mother would say, "You two! The war is at the front. You aren't supposed to be fighting here at home."

"Who's fighting?" the men would say, and clap each other on the back.

As they bantered on, I scratched Old Wolf's neck. "...make a farmer out of that little gal yet," I heard Tom Burt say. Well, I guess he did know I was there. I pulled my cap over my face and stuck out my tongue. I hated being called "that little gal." I was going on twelve, and the last thing I'd ever be was a farmer. But

I did like my time in the garden with Dad. I wanted to get back to it.

I moved my fingers inside my pocket, wishing the man would leave. He had taught us about tomatoes, true. Except for one thing. One secret we had learned not from Tom Burt but, in a way, from his wife, a woman as small and gentle as her husband was big and rough.

The men's voices droned on in quiet conversation, their teasing over for now.

"How's Mrs. Burt?"

"Fine. Heard from the boy?" The only time Tom Burt's tone softened was when he asked about my brother, Jeff, almost as though he missed him, too.

"Not in a while." Dad folded his arms and looked at the ground.

"We'll get this war over soon," Burt said.

It was a conversation I heard wherever I went with my father. When was "soon"? I wondered.

Tom Burt left, Old Wolf leaping out ahead of him, and we went back to our tomatoes. As our hands danced quietly among the leaves, I found myself counting the blossoms. Then the numbers became days. How many days do wars last? I wondered. How many gardens, how many more years before Jeff would be here again?

At last we reached the end of the row. I rolled up my cap and stuck it in my hip pocket as we walked up the back steps. Stillness had come over Dad. It was not about the tomatoes, I knew.

There had been no letter from Jeff in a long time.

CHAPTER 2

The war had come as a surprise to some, but not to Jeff and my father. Long before our country got into it, the two of them had followed the overseas news. They leaned in toward the radio, elbows on knees, for the evening news with Lowell Thomas, then talked it over at supper. Both Nazi Germany and Japan had fired on U.S. ships at sea, trying to destroy the food we sent to England and China.

Our government had said that if Americans planted more home gardens, the crops from large farms could go to help our allies overseas. Mother hoped that would keep our boys out of the war—boys like Jeff and his friends. President Franklin Delano Roosevelt had approved a peacetime military draft, and Jeff was almost old enough to go.

So we planted our first garden ever in the spring of 1941, months before Japan plunked us into the war we didn't want. Naturally old Tom Burt was standing over us, giving advice.

The tomatoes were Jeff's idea. He sowed the seeds, small as coarse grains of sand, in boxes made from scrap wood and set them under the workroom window. The sun shone through the limbs of the mulberry tree, leaving the glass cold but warming the seeds.

When the tomato seeds sprouted into plants, Jeff and Dad set them out in the garden. Jeff told the old man looking over their shoulders, "Just wait till these get ripe, Mr. Burt. They'll be even better than yours!"

That made old Burt snort. "We'll just see about that."

Jeff never did get his ripe tomatoes. The tomatoes in Kansas still had months to go when, far out in the Atlantic Ocean, a German U-boat sank an American merchant ship. Jeff didn't wait to turn draft age. He enlisted on a clear June day, shortly after he graduated from Shady Grove High School.

I didn't cry until later. We were all brave at the train depot. Jeff hugged us and joked with Dad, "You gotta save my face here, Dad. Make sure those tomatoes beat old Tom Burt's."

Well, I didn't give a hoot about tomatoes. What were the tomatoes without Jeff? He had always been there, and now he was gone. I slouched on the back steps, wishing he would come around the corner of the house and call me "squirt." I dreamed of flying down the street on his handlebars, the way I had since before I could tie my shoes.

I didn't climb the mulberry tree. I let my library book go overdue. I watched Dad loosen soil with a hoe and bend over to pull out weeds or pick off bugs, but I didn't go help him. The garden had not kept Jeff at home. I wanted nothing to do with it.

"I don't see why we have to feed England and China," I burst out at supper one night.

Dad knew what I meant. "Jeff always wanted to join up, Teresa. He just left a little early, that's all." But I heard a catch in his voice and saw tears in my mother's eyes.

The first letter from Jeff came to all of us, but his second one was just for me. *Guess you'll have to eat my tomatoes while I'm away, squirt,* he wrote.

Jeff's tomatoes. Not England's, not China's.

The next day I sidled up to Dad in the garden. Soon we were watching together for the tiny green beads, no bigger than the ones on Mother's good necklace, to form inside the yellow tomato blossoms.

Old Tom Burt needled Dad into a regular duel over those tomatoes. Jeff had thrown down a dare, and Burt wasn't about to let it go. Word got around, and the neighbor ladies, with my mother and Mrs. Burt, ran blind taste tests. Late that first summer they pronounced the Markses' tomatoes a little bit better. "Oh, well, a little bit," Burt had sputtered. The *Chronicle,* our local paper, told it this way: "First-Time Gardener Beats Old-Timer."

Vegetables from that first garden sat on pantry shelves in Mason canning jars before our country ever got into the war. And just when our thoughts had started to turn to Christmas that year, Japanese planes bombed

7

an American naval base at Pearl Harbor, Hawaii. President Roosevelt went on the radio and called it "a date which will live in infamy." The United States was now in the war that had already spread across much of the world. Jeff had been gone for six months.

I took his place at the radio with Dad, listening for news of the war. It didn't go very well for our side for a long time. We damaged some German U-boats in the Atlantic, but it was a different story in the Pacific.

Right away the Kansas City paper screamed a headline: "Japanese Gain Quick Success." Hong Kong fell, then Singapore, and the Solomon Islands came under attack. Dad marked all these places on the map Jeff had made while he was still in school. Roosevelt called for sixty thousand airplanes to be built in one year. Wouldn't Jeff love that? Sixty thousand! I couldn't imagine *one* thousand.

Tom Burt demanded a rematch when we put in our second garden four months after Pearl Harbor, in the spring of '42. I guess we showed him! We beat him again.

We were heavy into the war by then, already feeling a food shortage that would get worse as the war went on and farmworkers left the fields to help build ships and airplanes.

A lot of people who had never gardened before began to dig up their yards. Victory gardens sprouted all over our town, and every town nationwide. Everyone said the gardens would help to bring the boys home. I tried hard to believe.

CHAPTER 3

The war news was better now, in the spring of 1943. According to the newsreels, the Allies were calling the shots, but we sure hadn't won yet.

I knew in my heart that Jeff was safe. Pilots were up above the fighting, weren't they? It was just that he was gone.

I tried to be happy, because he was flying and that's what he'd always wanted to do. I tried not to be happy that he wasn't a marine. That didn't seem right, not when I thought about Wake Island out in the Pacific, and our marines who had met with a brutal defeat there. Jeff would be back someday. Sonny Ferguson, the judge's son, would never come home again.

But I wasn't thinking about Sonny Ferguson, or even

about the war, when the jangle of the telephone broke in on our Sunday breakfast. I was thinking about the lace on my new dress. Mother had spent extra money on the lace, and extra time to sew it on. I ate in my bathrobe, all dressed except for the blue watered taffeta that would be my good dress until I outgrew it.

"On Sunday morning?" Mother said when the telephone rang.

I was closest to it. I heard the shaking in Mrs. Burt's voice. "Teresa? Please, can your daddy come quickly? Mr. Burt's been badly hurt."

"Yes!" I dropped the receiver and echoed her words.

The next part was a blur: siren squealing, neighbors spilling into the street, the doctor saying stand back, stand back. The men carried him out, big Tom Burt, a helpless giant on a canvas stretcher. The ambulance sped away for the nearest hospital, fifty miles east. I glimpsed Mrs. Burt sitting in the back, a tiny figure squeezed in on a stool beside the stretcher. I wanted to take back all the bad stuff I had thought about Mr. Burt.

It was too late for church. Neighbors milled about, then drifted in shock back to their homes. "We'd better close up their house," said Dad.

We shut the windows, pulled down the shades and turned off the stove burner under the coffeepot, then walked back across the street in silence, Old Wolf whimpering beside us. We sat on our porch, me in my bathrobe, Mother and Dad still dressed for church, staring across at the empty house.

"Mr. Burt was out visiting his old farm," Mother

said. "The tractor turned over on him. Lucas, the hired man, brought him in."

Like many older town folk, the Burts had rented their country land to younger farmers, then retired from the grinding work of putting in crops year after year. Lucas had stayed on, working for the new tenants.

"Mr. Burt took to town life with all the willingness of a plow mule," Dad said, smiling at some memory. "He spends enough time in his garden to bring in sixty acres of wheat. Says a man isn't made for sitting around the house."

"I guess that's what kept drawing him back to the country," said Mother. "He just had to be back in the fields now and then."

I looked across at Mr. Burt's garden and wondered if Dad was thinking the same thing I was.

The sun crept behind the mulberry tree before we started Sunday dinner. We said little as we ate. The chicken my mother had killed and dressed on Saturday—I had plucked out the last stubborn pinfeathers myself—was fried to a golden crispness, but it felt strange in my mouth. Even the meat of the wishbone, which I no longer had to fight Jeff for, tasted dry.

"They'll have him more comfortable by now," Dad said.

"I know," I said, guilty that my thoughts were not with Mr. Burt. I was thinking of his wife. Gas rationing would not allow her to travel back and forth while Mr. Burt lay in the hospital. She would stay with friends in the city. It would be a long stay, I feared.

I missed her already. I could still see her in the ambulance as it pulled away. How could the man and his wife be so different? I wondered. One look from Tom Burt could scare the socks off you. Yet I'd had wonderful hours with Mrs. Burt among her flowers. In winter, when there were no flowers to pick, we sat in her kitchen with steaming cups of hot chocolate, talking and watching snowflakes gather at the window.

I had promised to feed and walk Old Wolf until the Burts' relatives could come from Morris County to take him to their farm. We'd already locked up their house. That took care of everything but the garden. "I can water the flowers after school," I said as we cleared the dishes. "School's out soon, anyway."

I could not imagine taking care of Mr. Burt's enormous vegetable garden. Even so, I was stunned when Dad said, "I'll call Lucas to come and plow it under."

"Daddy, you can't do that!" I blurted out, even though he was talking to Mother.

"It's the way Mr. Burt wants it, Teresa."

I forgot that I had once hated the thought of gardening and that I didn't exactly love old man Burt. "But that garden is his reason for being!" I exclaimed. Mrs. Burt had told me that, in those very words.

Dad looked up, surprised but firm.

"Tom's a proud man. He doesn't want to come home and see his garden dried up."

"Alan, couldn't we take care of it?" my mother asked.

"I don't see how," he said. "We're stretched thin as it is, without help at the store."

I knew he was right. The war had drawn workers away from small towns, to the army, to farms and to factories in the cities. Dad worked long hours at our store, Marks Bootery. There were more old shoes to fix than new ones to sell during these war days, and his repairman had left for the airplane factory. Mother worked there, too, while I was in school, and brought bookkeeping home at night.

It was the same for everybody in town.

"What about Lucas?" I asked.

"Lucas has his hands full out at the farm."

"Dad—" I began.

He held up a hand. "Tom Burt has planted that whole empty lot next to his house. We could never do it justice."

"But you can't just destroy it!"

"Teresa, Mr. Burt is a farmer. Farmers plow things under sometimes. When they do, the plants nourish the soil for the next crop."

I frowned. "What did you tell him?" I asked.

"I said, 'I'll take care of it, Tom Burt. You just get well.' "

I turned my head and risked a smile. He hadn't actually said we would plow it under.

Upstairs, I brushed my hair one hundred strokes and pulled on my pajamas. I wished I could talk to Jeff about the garden.

It wasn't just Mr. Burt's reason for being. It was his reason for challenging Dad. I knew by now that he did it to help Dad bear the time without Jeff. I'd watched

Dad a lot. When he dug his hands into the soil, or smoothed the dirt over a weeded place, he had a peaceful look about him. I think he felt close to Jeff in the garden. I did, with the sky there above us. Even if miles and miles away, Jeff was in that same sky, flying his B-24.

I mumbled a short version of my prayers, skipping the kneeling part but not skipping "God bless Jeff" (and of course my folks and the Burts), and curled around my pillow. I don't remember the words, but I think I asked how we could save the Burts' garden.

By morning I had the answer. But I would need a lot of help!

CHAPTER 4

At school I fidgeted all through the morning and afternoon. Finally last period came, and with it my favorite subject, current events. It was the moment I'd been waiting for.

"Who remembers what we were going to talk about today?" Miss Elliott had a great way of smiling when she asked a question. I flung my arm up. "Teresa?" she said.

"About how we can earn money over the summer for the war bond drive." At school we competed to see which grade could buy the most savings stamps with money the kids earned themselves. I raced on so that no one could break in. "And I have a way."

"Good. Tell us." Miss Elliott folded her arms and leaned against her desk.

"We can tend Mr. Tom Burt's garden while he's in the hospital." I had already told them about the terrible accident and that Mr. Burt would be away a long time. "Then, when the vegetables get ripe, we can sell them."

Maria, who was supposed to be my best friend, just stared at her hands, folded in a tight knot on her desk.

Andy Jones, who sat behind me, sputtered, "Garden work? Forget it! My dad makes me do that at home."

"Ick, I hate the bugs and worms," said Ellie White.

"Bad idea," said Billy Riggs, who almost never joined in class discussions. "Old man Burt is mean as the—"

"Billy." Miss Elliott gave him a look.

"Dickens."

"He is not!" Here I was, defending the man I myself thought was gruff and unfriendly. But one thing I knew: Billy Riggs had no room to talk about being mean.

He was the new kid in town, sort of. He'd come after the school year started. At first he was okay. Everybody made over him because he was new, and Miss Elliott went out of her way. That part kind of made me jealous. After all, the rest of us had been in this school since first grade.

After a while Billy began to ignore the kids who tried to be friends with him. He'd grunt or shrug or walk away. Later, he made fists, and now he was getting into fights. Miss Elliott might just have been glad he was absent as much as he was.

"What do you think, class?" asked Miss Elliott. "What do you know about gardens?"

"I help my granddad dig potatoes," one boy said.

"Digging's not the same as raising," Rich Gibbons said with authority. "It takes a lot of work to raise a garden up to the picking stage."

"What kind of work?" Miss Elliott asked.

They had answers.

"You have to pull a thousand weeds."

"And water, when it doesn't rain."

"Look for bugs."

"And when it's time to pick, you have to pick, right then. If you don't and it rains, things can rot."

Miss Elliott summed up. "Then it's largely a matter of watching for what needs to be done and doing it at the right time, isn't it?"

The class agreed.

"Who would do that? Who would do the watching?"

"My father and I." I hadn't intended to volunteer Dad, but surely he could take time for inspections.

"And once you know what to do, who will do it?" Miss Elliott wanted to know.

"Us kids," I said.

"What if we kill the guy's garden?" someone asked.

"Huh!" Billy Riggs looked up suddenly from the doodle he was making on his red tablet cover. "He'll kill *you*!"

Best ignore him. "There's something else," I said. The *Chronicle* had challenged the whole town to compete in the Great Tomato Duel, as they called Dad's contest with Mr. Burt. "The newspaper is giving a prize for the best tomatoes this year. Anyone can enter. Maybe we could win a whole bond!"

"Maybe we're getting ahead of ourselves," Miss Elliott said, cutting me off. "Teresa, do you have the Burts' permission to sell their garden produce?"

"Permission?"

She pressed me. "Have you asked them about this?"

I swallowed. "Not yet."

"And your father?"

"No. But he'll say yes." I tried to sound confident, although I wasn't at all sure.

"Why don't we think about it," Miss Elliott suggested, "and talk again tomorrow?"

She unfolded her arms and studied her watch. "Remember, I'll be gone all summer, working on my father's farm. So you children will be on your own. You'd better talk with your parents."

I gave my best smile to the class. Then I bit my lower lip.

"You're nuts," Maria said on the walk home.

"I know." I dropped her off at her house and kept on going instead of stopping to gab. Old Wolf was waiting for his walk.

The dog paced back and forth, whining at the fence that held him captive in the Burts' side yard. When I unlatched the gate, he jumped up, nearly knocking me over.

"Easy, Wolfie," I said as I snapped a leash to his collar. "You miss them, don't you?" He strained at the leash and barked at something in the alley. I looked up just in time to see the tail end of Billy Riggs ducking behind the shed. "Never mind, Wolfie," I said. "He's just taking the alley way home."

I could barely keep up with the bounding dog. I hoped the relatives who would be coming for him the next day would remember to exercise him, and to brush that thick yellow-brown coat. When I got him back to my room, where he'd be sleeping again that night, I couldn't wait to sit down, even if it was for homework.

My desk, by an upstairs window, overlooked the front walk. When Dad and Mother strode into view, I dashed down the stairs. Wolfie followed me.

"Daddy!" I called as he came through the door.

Before I could say more, he said, "I need to talk with you, Teresa. Sit down." He remained standing and loosened his necktie. "I understand you have taken it upon yourself to involve me in this."

I knew what "this" meant. "You know about it?"

"The phone at the store has been ringing off the hook. Didn't we decide last night that we would honor Mr. Burt's wishes?"

That wasn't exactly the way I remembered it. "I thought—"

I thought the garden could be saved. I thought Mr. Burt would like that, no matter what he said. I thought Mrs. Burt would like it, too. Something inside me said that keeping his garden alive would bring Mr. Burt back, like the victory gardens would bring the boys back.

I began again. "What if we could do a good job?"

Dad frowned. "That's not the point, Teresa. The point is you went off on your own after we had talked about this. And you involved me without asking."

I hadn't meant to do that, but my idea must be important if so many people had called. I studied a worn spot on the rug.

He sighed his I-am-trying-to-understand sigh. A good sign.

"How do you plan to make it work?" he said at last.

"I thought you and I could decide what needs to be done," I explained, "and we kids could divide up the work."

"Is this what you volunteered me for?"

"Will you do it?"

"I don't know, Teresa. I hate to go against Tom Burt's wishes."

Mother had been listening quietly. "Perhaps Mr. Burt's wish was simply not to put anyone out. He's an independent man. He may find it hard to accept favors."

"But he does favors," I said. At least for grown-ups.

"All the time," Mother said.

"He's the one who taught us to garden!" I said.

Dad smiled at last. "Indeed. He even challenged me to that first tomato duel just to make me stay with it." He rubbed his chin. I knew he was thinking about Jeff.

"So it's okay? If it's okay with Mrs. Burt?"

"We can think about it," he said. "I hope you know what you're getting into, Miss Marks."

I bounded out of my chair and back up to the desk. I couldn't wait to tell Jeff. I pulled a thin sheet of V-mail letter paper from the desk drawer and filled in Jeff's name and address in the box at the top marked To, and my own where it said From. I wrote the date, May 11, 1943.

Dear Jeff,

Mr. Burt's in the hospital, badly hurt. He's going to be okay, though. Mother's writing you with the details. He said to plow his garden under. I didn't think we should (do you?) because the government says we need gardens to help win the war, and because he loves his garden. I'm going to take care of it if some kids at school will help me.

That would mean the tomato duel is between me and Dad this year, wouldn't it? Imagine me as old man Burt (giggle). I don't know what to do about the secret weapon.

I listen to the war news and I read Life *magazine, so I know where your kind of plane goes. I cut stories out and put them in a scrapbook to show you after the war. Then you can tell me whether you were there.*

Please tell me more about flying. What's it really like up there? Are you ever scared?

A V-mail letter was just one page long. I'd run out of space, so I squeezed in *I miss you. Love, Teresa*, then folded the sheet and licked the flap.

"I'll leave early in the morning, go by the post office, and then over to school," I said, as if to Jeff. I patted Wolfie on the head. "I'll go crazy waiting for last period."

CHAPTER 5

We were chattering around Miss Elliott's desk when the tardy bell rang. She had to shoo us to our seats for the flag salute.

I felt pride as I recited it. The pledge reminded me of what Jeff was fighting for—liberty and justice for all. Other kids in school had brothers away. Uncles, cousins, even fathers were gone.

The gardens were only a part of the war effort at home. We saved tinfoil and string, wore out our clothes and walked holes in our shoe soles. At school we skimped on paper, because the government needed so much of it to print stamp books. Some of those books we emptied; others we filled.

We emptied the ration books, tearing out coupons

smaller than postage stamps to give to the grocer along with our money. Some stamps were for meat, others for sugar, coffee or canned goods. Separate books rationed gasoline. It was a lot to keep track of.

The back of the ration books said: *IMPORTANT: Salvage TIN CANS and WASTE FATS. They are needed to make munitions for our fighting men.* We did that, and more.

Then there were the books we filled. On Fridays Miss Elliott put a Mason jar on her desk. With every dime we dropped into it, we bought a red savings stamp with a soldier on it. Stamp by stamp, we licked and stuck until our war bond booklets bulged. With luck I would have all 185 ten-cent stamps by the end of summer, and then I could trade my book in for a bond. In ten years, with interest, it would be worth twenty-five dollars to help pay for college.

We didn't go right into reading after the flag salute. Instead Miss Elliott said, "Let's hear more about your summer plans."

I held my breath as hands flew up and the kids called out their moneymaking schemes.

"The neighbor will pay me to help with her canning."

"Mr. Perkins says all the teenagers will be working on farms. He'll need a kid at the IGA grocery to sweep and shelve canned goods."

"I work for my dad in the summer, painting houses. I get to do the porch railings."

Others planned to water yards, mow lawns, baby-sit, run errands, do dishes or dust houses, but not all the talk was of work. We'd be roller-skating, riding bikes and flying kites, too, and sprinting through water sprinklers on hot afternoons and catching fireflies at night. I could hardly wait.

I listened as Miss Elliott drew everyone out. Only Billy Riggs seemed to have no interest in summer. I saw him slumped in his seat, doodling in the margins of his arithmetic book. Miss Elliott was always pretty patient with Billy, considering he never did anything but draw war pictures: Swastika-decorated tanks with guns spitting bullets or bayonets dripping blood, enough to make you sick.

When no one mentioned the garden, I knew I had to speak up.

"I still want to work in Mr. Burt's garden," I said, trying to sound excited.

Miss Elliott glanced expectantly from pupil to pupil.

I kept talking, thinking how Tom Sawyer had gotten Ben Rogers and all those others to whitewash Aunt Polly's fence. He told his friends a boy didn't get a chance to whitewash every day. Make the thing difficult to attain, Mark Twain wrote.

"You don't get a chance like this every day," I said. "The garden is already planted, and the food will all be ours. To sell! For money!" Then I added the clincher, I thought. "But of course we can't use too many people. We'd all be bumping into each other."

No hands waved.

"The downtown merchants will join together to donate one stamp for every stamp we buy with money from the garden," I said. I crossed my fingers in case it

was a lie, but the merchants had done such things before.

Andy Jones jumped to his feet. "Let's just take their
stamps and forget about the work!"

For once I appreciated Andy's clowning. The kids
laughed and sat up a little straighter.

"Who wants to help Teresa with the garden?" asked
Miss Elliott.

I was surprised at the first volunteer.

"I will." It was Rich Gibbons, who had claimed to
know all about gardening. I hoped he did.

When Rich volunteered, Louise Lang quickly followed. I smiled.

The next one surprised me even more.

"Me too," said Andy. "Better than doing it at home."

Then Maria raised her hand. Even if you are nuts,
her grin told me.

"Count me in," said Scott Walker. "My mom says it's
the decent thing to do." I swallowed hard. Scott's father
was away. He had volunteered after Sonny Ferguson
was killed in action.

Miss Elliott wrote their names on the blackboard.
"Who else?" she asked.

The biggest surprise was yet to come. Squeamish
Ellie White stood up and said, "I guess I like money
more than I hate bugs."

I was grinning now. "Good! Everybody meet me at
the Burts' garden, across the street from my house, on
Thursday after school."

I skipped all the way home, my friend Maria beside
me, barely keeping up. "Can you come over?" I asked her.

I wouldn't be walking Old Wolf. Mr. Burt's relatives had come for him that morning. Besides, with a stiff breeze blowing out of the south, it was a perfect day for flying the kite Dad and I had put together over the weekend.

"Sure."

We finished tying white rags to the tail string and tried to launch the kite. I tossed it up while she let out the string; then we tried it the other way around, but each time the kite sank back down to the ground. Laurence Coffey came delivering the *Chronicle* just as we were about to give up.

"Want some help?" he asked.

"Hey, Kuppa. Yeah!" I said. Laurence Coffey had been stuck with his nickname longer than anyone could remember. His senior class was down from forty-two to thirty, only eight of them boys, so many had already gone off to war.

"How's your brother, Teresa? Flying rings around them Natzees?" At least Kuppa wasn't as somber as Mr. Burt.

"Good, far as I know," I said.

"I'll be going, too. Soon as school's out."

"You've been drafted?"

"Nah. Wait for the draft, you're cannon fodder. Enlist and you can get what you want. Me, I want navy. Hold or fly?"

"Fly," I said, and handed him the stick with the kite string wound around it.

"Okay. Before you take it up, face it into the wind. Say 'go.' "

"Go!" I tossed the kite.

Kuppa ran a few steps, letting the string out gradually as the wind caught the kite and lifted it.

"You got it!" Maria called.

"Gotta go," Kuppa said. He handed me the string and took off with his papers.

The kite dipped. I tightened up on the string, then felt a strong tug as it fluttered in the wind. My spirits soared with it. The sky was blue, the air hovered right between warm and cool, and I couldn't imagine any place nicer. I wondered what the kids overseas were doing right now. Were they flying kites? Or fleeing to air raid shelters?

"Do you ever think about why we were born in this country instead of where the war is?" I asked Maria, passing the string to her for a turn.

She gave me a strange look and no answer, but it was a good question, one I had asked myself over and over.

We hadn't taken time for a snack. "You hungry?" I asked her after a while.

"Starved."

We reeled the kite in and headed for the kitchen. I spread peanut butter on crackers while Maria filled two glasses with cold milk from the bottle. We took them to the dining room table.

"What in the world is that?" Maria asked, nodding at the map on the wall.

"That *is* the world," I said, laughing. "It's been there all along."

"Never noticed. Looks like we're in school."

"We moved it down from Jeff's room after Pearl Harbor. Dad mounted it on pasteboard from grocery boxes so we could stick pins in it, see? He marks the battle sites on it."

Maria shrugged. She wasn't very interested in the war, but I could see why. She was the oldest child in her family, always taking care of the babies, as she called her little brothers. The only reason she wasn't home with them that afternoon was that her mother didn't have to work that day. She did take a second look at the map, though.

"It looks different from the one at school somehow."

"It is," I said, trying to spark her interest. "That was Jeff's idea. He made it to mark the flights of famous aviators, but it works to follow the war, too. Better than the one at school, I think."

"Why?"

"Remember when Miss Elliott said a world map is made by opening up the globe and stretching it out flat?"

"Uh-huh."

"Well, if you open it up at a different place, the United States is in the middle, here." I pointed. "Now you can see where the war regions are in relation to us, one on each side. Japan on this side"—I stretched out my left arm—"and Europe on the other. Makes it easier to keep track of what's going on where."

"What's all that stuff on it?"

"Flags. See?" I touched a small piece of blue, shaped like a V and flying from under the head of a pin stuck into the map.

"Rickrack?"

"Yes. The blue is for our side, the Allies. I tried cutting little shapes out of paper, but they just tore. Mother came up with the rickrack, from her sewing box."

"Not bad. What's the red for?"

"The Japanese."

"There are two flags here, one red and one blue. Why?"

"Wake Island," I said. "The Japanese still hold it, and we're still trying to get it back."

"Oh, right," said Maria. After a moment she added, "That was where Sonny Ferguson was killed. I really didn't know him." More than a year had passed since Shady Grove's first gold star went up in the Fergusons' window, making the war so real, so terrible.

"Neither did I, but Jeff did. And everybody knows Sonny's father, the judge."

"They say they didn't find out where he died until later."

"I heard that. Another marine came to town and told them, somebody who had fought alongside Sonny."

"And they couldn't send his body home, but his folks felt better just knowing where it—where he—oh!" Maria put her hand over her mouth.

I knew what she was thinking. "Jeff is in the air," I said. "Marines fight on the ground."

She was anxious to change the subject. "Two flags on Japan, too. Why?"

"We bombed Tokyo a year ago. See?" I read from the faded clipping I had taped to the edge of the map: " 'Doolittle's B-25s Bomb Tokyo.' Jimmy Doolittle was one of Jeff's pilot heroes. That's why I saved the article." We had caught the Japanese completely by surprise. The writer called it stranger than fiction. The enemy thought our planes couldn't get all the way across the ocean to reach them. They were right, but we launched our bombers from the USS *Hornet* in the middle of a raging sea.

"Wow. But look here." Maria waved a finger over the red flags pinned to islands in the Pacific Ocean. "Haven't we captured anything? The newsreels keep saying we're so good."

"We are. Dad says our forces are far superior." I pointed to an island in the ocean between Alaska and Japan. "Here's something we captured. Amchitka."

"What good is that?"

"Very good. We could bomb Japan easily from there."

"I thought we'd already bombed them."

I sighed. Maria was smart, but she didn't know much about wars.

"I should go now," she said. I walked her to the door and said goodbye.

After I saw her out, I sipped at the last of my milk and stared at the map. On the right-hand side, black flags—black for the Axis swastika—dotted most of Europe, where Germany had overrun its neighbors. One blue flag, however, pinned to Stalingrad in Russia, told a different story. It marked the place where one of Hitler's huge armies had finally met defeat.

Jeff's dotted lines were still there, where he had traced historic flights, like Amelia Earhart's solo flight from Hawaii to California, and those of Charles "Lucky Lindy" Lindbergh and Billy Mitchell.

Maybe it was reading about Mitchell that had made Jeff so sure we would get into another war and that air power would decide the winner. "Do you know Mitchell was court-martialed for saying that?" Jeff had told us at supper one night. "They said he disgraced the army."

Billy Mitchell had died five years before Pearl Harbor, but some of his predictions came true. His friend Hap Arnold, who had learned to fly from the famous Orville Wright, was now General H. H. Arnold, chief of the U.S. Army Air Forces. Jeff had always dreamed of flying with Hap Arnold, and now, in a way, he was.

Lucky him. I ran my finger across the map and traced my own dream. Someday I would take a train from Kansas to New York City. Then I'd fly across the ocean to Sicily, that island at the toe of the boot of Italy, and sail across the Mediterranean Sea to North Africa. There wouldn't be any war then, and the water would be peaceful and as blue as my taffeta dress.

CHAPTER 6

Andy Jones sank to the sidewalk, cross-legged, and draped his wrists over his folded knees. "I don't know," he said. "This is huge."

The kids had come, sure enough, on Thursday after school. Andy wasn't the only one with a long face.

"Yeah, is it a garden or a farm?"

"Where do we start?"

"My dad will show us," I said. "But first we have to have a plan." I held up a tablet and pencil.

We managed to agree on three things. I listed them and made a five-line star in front of each one.

☆ WORK THURSDAYS AFTER SCHOOL TILL SUMMER
☆ WORK SATURDAYS, NOW AND ALL SUMMER
☆ PICK, SELL, AND DELIVER

Andy added a fourth:

★ NO ADULTS ALLOWED, EXCEPT FOR ADVICE

"That way they'll be dying to help us," he said. "Do we sign in blood?"

"Yeah, yours," said Rich.

Scott hung around after the others left. He seemed to have something to say that he didn't want everyone to hear. He still held the hoe, shifting it from hand to hand.

"Heard from your dad?" I asked, not knowing what else to say.

"Not in a while," he said. I felt like we had suddenly become the adults.

"How's your mother doing?" It was my way of asking how Scott was, how they were all holding up. It was the same thing people asked me sometimes.

"Good, I guess. She's making a garden, too, her first one. I think she dreaded it at the beginning, but she said since the baby was older now, she should do it, like everyone else."

"To bring the boys home sooner?"

"And the men."

I swallowed, embarrassed by my blunder. It was hard enough to have a brother gone. What must it be like for Scott?

"Some folks don't understand that."

"What?"

"That my dad left." He scratched a line in the dirt with the hoe.

"But he's serving his country! The whole town's proud of him."

"Some. Not all. People say things."

"What people?"

"The old maid, for one."

"Theda Buell? Phoo. Nobody listens to her."

"Maybe you're right. Maybe people just don't know what to say. They kind of hush up when we come around. Or they talk low, like they don't know I'm listening."

"Same here. People talk to my mother while I'm standing right there. 'Of course, Teresa's so much younger.' As if I don't miss Jeff just because there aren't any others between him and me. I miss him more that way. I'm the only kid at home now."

"I know." Scott gripped the hoe's handle with both hands and finally said what was on his mind. "Sometimes I won't be able to come. When one of the little kids gets sick, I take care of the others. If Mom gets sick, I take care of them all."

Who would be ashamed of that? I wondered. He must have read the question in my look. "I'm not sure the guys would understand," he said.

Probably they wouldn't, I thought as he pedaled away on his bike. Not many boys become man of the house before they're through being boys.

Maria and Ellie helped with little kids, too. All the boys had yards to mow. I had only to keep the living room straight and help with the cooking and dishes. If the war had made Scott a man of the house, it had made me an only child, for now. I drew in a huge breath. This garden would be mostly up to me.

At home, Mother sat at the sewing machine, leaning

over a swath of purple checks. "One more sleeve to set in," she said. "You'll look nice in this."

I was eager for it to be finished. A new school dress so late in the year was unusual, but my old ones were patched, faded and way up past my knees.

Mother did her sewing in scraps of time trimmed out of the late afternoon, after work and before supper. She said sewing wasn't work, it was sitting down. I believed her. She had a contented look just then. I thought perhaps I shouldn't disturb her mood, but I had something on my mind.

"Have you ever heard anything bad about Mr. Walker, Scott's dad?"

"Bad? Like what?"

"Like something about his being in the army, away from his family?"

"Well, just that. But who are others to say that's bad? It's between him and his family."

"Then people do talk?"

"Oh, honey, there are always people who talk, but not many. Scott senior is a fine man who loves his family enough to help keep our country safe for them. What most people say is that both he and Mrs. Walker are very brave and patriotic."

"Scott's brave, too."

Mother reached for my hand. "So are you, Teresa."

I didn't see how, but I squeezed her hand.

I looked around at the room, Jeff's old room. The sewing machine now stood on the desk that had seen piles of math papers and model airplane parts. I used to watch him cut the soft balsa wood and fit wings to fuse-lage, covering it all with tissue paper. He had mounted a B-24 on one wall, a great plane with a four-foot wingspan. "I'm going to fly a real one of these some-day," he had told me.

His bicycle stood in the very spot where he had left it. No one had had the heart to move it, even to dust-mop under its wheels. I saw myself on the handlebars, waving my arms like the prop for his plane, and tears started running down my face.

"Not so brave," I said, and wiped my nose on my arm.

Mother snipped the thread from a finished seam. She held the dress up to me, then gathered it and me into her arms. "God gave us tears," she said. "Sometimes they help to keep us brave." I couldn't imagine Mother crying, but at her words, I snuggled in.

Friday was another fidgety day. I dashed home from school, just in case Mrs. Burt called early with Mr. Burt's answer. The night before, when we had phoned to ask about Mr. Burt and to see whether we could keep the garden, she had said, "He's doing all right, but he'll be here a long time. I'm just not sure how he'll feel about the garden. I'd better call you back."

If only I could talk to Jeff. I checked the mailbox by the front door, hoping, hoping. It was there! A letter from Jeff, addressed to all of us in Jeff's familiar scrawl: *Mr. and Mrs. Alan Marks and Teresa.* That meant I could open it without waiting.

It's been a long time since I've written, Jeff began. It sure had been. Our letters often crossed in the mail, so he didn't know about Mr. Burt yet. *Dad, thanks for telling me about the map a while back. Save it for me. I read the* Army Times *when I can get it, but I can't keep up with everything like we used to. Don't worry about me. Except for missing all of you, I'm fine. Flying is hard work, but it beats anything else!*

Then came a special word to each of us. To me he wrote, *Well, squirt, I guess you're tall enough to ride my bike now. Ask Dad to lower the seat. Don't skin up his trees.* I laughed at that. He had once crashed into a slender Chinese elm that Dad had just planted. As Jeff told it, the tree got more sympathy than he did.

I dashed upstairs and changed out of my school dress into my overalls, then went into Jeff's room. It smelled of Mother's talcum powder now, instead of wood and airplane glue.

The bicycle leaned on its kickstand, dust gathered under its tires. I closed my fingers around the handlebars, eased the stand up with my foot, and stretched one leg over the crossbar. Yes, Dad would need to lower the seat, but I was tall enough. I wanted to ride it at once, only the tires needed air and the seat was too high. Plus I was waiting for Mrs. Burt's call.

So when the telephone rang downstairs, I scrambled off the bike and bounded down. It was for me, but it wasn't Mrs. Burt. It was Louise Lang, dropping out. "It's going to be too much work," she whined, "and my family already buys bonds."

"She's spoiled," I told Mother that night as we fixed supper.

"Perhaps. What about the others? Will they stay?"

I didn't have an answer yet.

The next call brought worse news, much worse. It came while we were eating. "Wait a few days," I heard my mother say into the phone. "He may come back. Let's not tell the Burts just yet." Old Wolf had run away from the Burts' relatives, just days after they had come for him.

I was edgy, waiting for Mrs. Burt to call. I picked at my supper and studied the telephone on the wall: brown wooden box with black crank, mouthpiece and receiver on its hook. It seemed to bring only bad news. Did I really want it to ring?

When it did, later, I answered nervously. We were in the workroom putting air in the bicycle tires with Jeff's old tire pump. This time it was Mrs. Burt calling. At least we would get it settled. Either we could do the garden or we couldn't.

I blurted out an awkward "How's Mr. Burt?"

"They're taking good care of him, dear," she said. "He says it's okay for you to take over the garden, on one condition. You have to beat Alan Marks in the tomato duel."

I blew out a long breath. Then I laughed. "Can I come live with you if we do?"

When I told Dad he grinned and said, "Impossible."

"Impossible you would let me move?"

"Impossible you'll beat me," he said. He screwed the cap back on the tire stem.

I shoved my hands into my overall pockets and made myself tall and gruff. "We'll just see about that, Alan Marks!"

That was how I took over more than an old man's garden. I took over his campaign to help my father get through the war.

On Saturday morning I tore away from the breakfast table with a slice of toast between my teeth. "I'll go wait for the kids," I mumbled around the toast.

"I'll be along," Dad said. He didn't mention that I hadn't asked to be excused. I guess he knew I was jittery.

When Andy and Rich clomped up the street with rakes and hoes from home, I grinned. Scott wheeled up on his bike. Ellie roller-skated over, and Maria walked the few blocks from her house. They called out to each other, like they hadn't just been together the day before at school.

Andy had an empty jar with holes in the lid.

"What's that for?" asked Ellie.

"Catchin' grasshoppers."

"What for?"

"Fun!"

"Also keeps them from eating the leaves," said my dad, who had followed me across the street.

The kids already knew Dad. "You sold me my shoes," said Rich.

"You only half-soled mine," said Andy. He laughed at his own joke.

We walked follow-the-leader-style, up and down the garden rows.

"What will these be?" Dad asked, pointing to lacy green sprouts in the first row.

"Carrots!" said Andy.

"How can you tell?"

"I saw the sign." We laughed. Mr. Burt had nailed brightly colored seed packets to sticks and stuck them in the ground.

"How soon will we have things to pick?" asked Scott.

"Depends. Mr. Burt staggers his planting so that he has something from the garden all summer. Some plants are already producing, and some are just young sprouts." Dad pulled up a small plant, tapped it to loosen the dirt, and held up the slender beginning of a red radish. "See, you have one crop coming in already."

We walked along every row, identifying the plants by the packets. Dad gave us the rundown on what to expect. Some crops were easier than others, he said. Some needed to be thinned. Some had to be checked every day. Some, like string beans, could almost raise themselves.

"Tomatoes take the most watching because they're slow to develop and have to be watered just so," he said.

"And there's a big tomato contest," said Andy. "A whole bond riding on it. Isn't that kind of weird?"

"You won't think so if you win it," Dad said, then teased, "But don't worry. I'll be the winner."

"Says you!" I said.

In the center of the garden was a sandstone slab, and on it a statue atop a stone base. "Be careful of Saint Francis here," said Dad. "Don't back into him with the handle of your hoe. The Burts set great store by this statue."

"Especially Mrs. Burt," I said. "She told me she almost cried when Mr. Burt gave it to her for their anniversary. She loves the bird in the saint's hand, and the words on the stone." From where I stood I couldn't see the prayer chiseled there, but I knew some of it: *Where there is hatred let me sow love; where there is injury, pardon.*

"I suggest you each choose a crop or two," said Dad. "Then you won't all have to worry about everything."

"Dibs on beans," said Andy, picking the easy one.

"Fine," said Dad. "Do some research on the crops you choose."

"Research?" said Andy.

"Find out things. Ask around, talk to people. A little information can save a lot of sweat."

I figured I had all the information about tomatoes that I would ever need, and because they took the most watching, I'd easily get my choice.

The garden had accumulated a week's worth of

weeds since Mr. Burt's accident. "The small ones come right out when you pull," said Dad, "but be sure to get all the root. If the weed is a big one, dig around it with your hoe or a trowel." He showed us. "Lift it out, root and all. Move it gently to the basket so its seeds won't scatter."

Then he rubbed the dirt from his hands and checked his pocket watch. "I'm off to work," he said. "You know what to do."

We looked at the garden and then at each other. It was as if our feet had grown their own roots. Then Dad called over his shoulder, "Oh, a message from Charley Sweet. Free cones at the Sweet Shoppe when you're done today."

Feet left the ground as everyone yelled, "Hurray!" "Yippee!" "Ice cream!"

We jabbered and jostled each other, pulling, hoeing, and filling the bushel basket with weeds.

Suddenly the mood changed. A rock thudded against the basket.

"Well, well, if it ain't the little gardeners!" We knew that voice without looking up.

"Billy Riggs! Get outta here!" yelled Andy.

"Ain't you the hee-roes!" Billy's taunt rang across the garden.

"Ignore him," I said. "He just wants attention."

"Well, he's gonna get it." Andy picked up a clod of dirt.

"Easy, Jones," said Scott. "Billy's mean. It's not worth it."

I knew Scott was right. Billy lived down beyond the depot, out past the junkyard. He passed my house on his way to school. I'd seen him cut through the Burts' garden, stomping on plants as he went, Old Wolf barking furiously at him from his pen.

Andy stood still, arm raised, fist clutching the clod.

"Dare ya!" Billy called.

Scott eased Andy's arm down. "He's full of baloney. Forget it," he said.

Andy dropped his arm, but Billy yelled again, "Sissy!"

None of us saw exactly what happened next. All at once, Billy was down and Andy was sitting on him, blood dripping from his nose onto Billy's shirt. We gasped when he held Billy by the hair and hit him in the face. Ellie squealed. Scott groaned.

"Quiet! People will hear you!" I said through gritted teeth.

It took all of us to pull Andy off.

"Whatsa matter, scared I'll take you, too?" Billy sneered at us. "I could've finished him."

"Get out," Andy said, "or I'll finish you."

Billy snorted. "Huh! You'd better eat your Wheaties first!"

It looked to me like Billy was the one who needed Wheaties. He left, pulling at his bloodied shirt and shouting over his shoulder, "My pop will kill you for this!"

CHAPTER 8

Andy wrapped his fist around a weed and slashed into its root with a trowel. "If that little runt shows up here again . . ." We were back in the garden, five days after the fight.

"Not likely," said Scott. "You licked him. Forget it."

But I could see they hadn't forgotten. They worked furiously on the garden, not about to be stopped by the likes of Billy Riggs.

To my surprise, they had already learned something about their plants. They'd asked at home, at the neighbors', at the greenhouse, anywhere they could. Some even looked in books. We talked as we worked, each of us trying to make our own choice look best.

"Lookee," Ellie sang. She pulled up a skinny radish. "My uncle loves these. He said he'd buy all I could pick."

"He'll have fire coming out of his head," said Andy, looking down the long row.

"Green peppers, too," said Ellie. "They look like toy ones! I'll still have these peppers when the radishes are gone. All I have to do is water."

I grinned. Ellie was having fun.

"Look here," I said. "Believe it or not, this is a tomato." I brushed the drying yellow petals away from a tight green ball. "We'll have tomatoes all summer once they get going."

Scott bent over the onions. "Onions and potatoes will keep in the ground right up until school starts."

"Hey, Scott, you could make soup. Wow, I love potato soup." That was Andy. He had chosen string beans because Dad had said they didn't take much work. I didn't think he'd done his research. He'd find out quickly enough that beans grow fast. Soon he'd have to pick every day.

Rich took the cabbage and leaf lettuce because they needed an experienced gardener, he said. "Lettuce wilts in the sun if you don't water it right. Cabbages get cabbage worms. You can't be squeamish about them." He tossed a glance at Ellie. When he looked away, she made a face.

Rich was almost as stuck-up as Louise had been, but I hoped his confidence would rub off on the rest of us.

Maria reached into a cluster of leaves on a thick vine to find a pea pod, stripped it open and ran her thumb along the inside. "See?" The peas were almost too small to see, but she popped them into her mouth.

Andy pointed in mock disgust. "She'll eat up all the profits!" he said.

If there are profits, I thought. There would soon be an avalanche of food, and I couldn't get a clear picture of how we would manage it.

We talked more than we worked, but that day's job was easy. We were finally ahead of the weeds.

Rich checked the angle of the afternoon sun. "Still time for a game," he said. "I've got the bat. Who's got the ball?"

"Me," said Andy. They had come prepared.

"Be sure the hoes are off the sidewalk and the blades turned down," I nagged. "We can come back for everything after the game."

"We need a decent name for this group," Andy said as we bolted for the empty corner lot down by the depot. "I'm going to croak if my dad says one more time, 'How're the little gardeners?' He's worse than Billy."

We tried some names, all of them bad. Grade School Gardeners? Famous Farmers? Shady Grove something—what begins with *S*?

"*Start*. Start the game," said Rich. "Let's name a pitcher."

"Me," said Scott and Andy together.

"Fine." Rich tossed the bat. Andy caught it by its middle and held it out to Scott, barrel down. They went hand over hand until Andy held it by the top. Fair and square. Scott settled for catcher.

"Four left. Three on base and a batter," I said. "Enough to play work-up." Andy handed the bat to Ellie. Maria, Rich, and I fanned out to cover the bases.

Ellie popped a fly ball on the first pitch, catching everybody by surprise. It barely cleared Rich's fingertips as he ran backward from second base, hand stretched up over his head.

We were wiping the sweat away when we trudged back and dropped to the grass under the Burts' giant elm. It was hot for May. The sun blazed, still not ready to sink behind the depot at the end of the next block. We cheered when Mother came over with cold lemonade.

"Something else," she said after we had all filled our cups. She held up a page of the *Chronicle*, just delivered to our door. "You're all famous."

Maria read the headline: " 'Young Sprouts Tend Young Sprouts.' "

We crowded around as Maria read on.

" 'Six brave youngsters have taken on Tom Burt's sprawling garden. Mr. Burt is recovering from injuries suffered in a tractor accident. Mrs. Burt reports to the *Chronicle* that he is doing well.

" 'Rumor has it that the kids are out to win the *Chronicle*'s Great Tomato Duel. That should make for some rivalry at neighbor Alan Marks's house. His daughter, Teresa, is one of the young gardeners. Others are . . .' " and their names were listed.

We read it again and repeated the headline, "Young Sprouts Tend Young Sprouts." Like it or not, we had our name.

By Saturday we were proud of it. Kids at school had crowded around us, and as word spread that we would sell our vegetables for war stamp money, merchants had called Dad to say they would help match our earnings. I hadn't told a lie!

We spread out and made short work of the weeds. They came out almost willingly, as a light rain during the night had done the watering for us.

Mother was at the dining table reading a letter when I came in from the garden.

"From Jeff?" I asked, although if I had looked at the envelope I would have known it wasn't.

"From Grandmother in Seattle," she said, meaning her mother. "I just finished." Her smile was bright, as if she had just had a long, happy visit with her family. "Here. Read it out loud to me. I want to hear it all again."

It was a long letter, the best kind.

> *We think of your Jeff every day. We do what we can for the war effort, as I know you do back there. Your sisters have both gone into war work, Christine. My oh my, women never did that in my day, but how I admire them. We are a more spread-out family than ever now. Jane has gone down to San Diego and works in an aircraft factory. Can you believe that slip of a girl drives rivets into airplanes? She says you should see the planes, huge ones, all lined up in double rows going down as far as the eye can see, all under one big high roof.*
>
> *Lizbeth works in the commercial tomato fields*

down in California's Central Valley. She says they've been told that their tomatoes go overseas to the troops. They say the tomatoes are good for the pilots' night vision. I thought Teresa would want to know that. Tell her to keep up the good work with those tomatoes at home. How I wish I could see her!

Dad's still a spotter. He knows the look of every enemy plane, although he's never spotted one flying over. I roll bandages for the Red Cross. It's not a lot, but every little bit helps, we hope.

You asked if we were still frightened up here. No. I admit we were shocked last year to learn that Japanese troops were in Alaska, but the newspapers may have overreported that. The Japanese weren't in mainland Alaska, you know, but on two small islands, quite far away.

"She means Kiska and Attu," I said, looking up at the map on the wall, then read on.

It would take better bombers than Japan has to get clear over here. Still, it was closer than anyone would like (except the Japanese!). As you will have heard, we're safe now. I've enclosed a news story in case you haven't seen it.

In fact, I had that story in Jeff's scrapbook, because B-24s helped at both islands. I read it again from Grandmother's clipping and shivered. *Last week U.S.*

troops were climbing the jagged snow-covered peaks of Attu Island, digging out the remnants of the Jap occupation force. Tokyo admitted the island was lost. Once more I was glad Jeff did his fighting in the air.

"When will we go see Grandmother?" I asked. I knew the answer, but I asked anyhow.

"After the war," my mother said. I noticed she didn't say "soon." I loved the story she had told since I was a little girl about how we happened to be in Kansas. I coaxed it out of her again.

"I met your father when he visited relatives in Seattle. It must have been fate. We met on a city bus. I learned he was a Kansas boy. Before you know it, I was a Kansas girl." Her eyes shone. "We always intended to go back out west for a visit, but there was never enough money or enough time, what with starting the store and all."

"Jeff and I were the 'all,' weren't we?" I teased her.

"You and Jeff will always be the all to your father and me."

I recited the rest for her: "Then this war came along."

She nodded. "But we'll go someday. You'll see."

$\mathcal{I}$ was just easing the dauber into the shoe polish when the door at the front of the Bootery squeaked open and clacked shut.

"Just me, not a customer," Maria called.

"In here!" I answered her.

We were in the back room—Mother, Dad and I. On

Saturday nights, when the stores stayed open late, we brought supper from home. After we ate, I polished my shoes for Sunday at Dad's repair table. For three cents a pair I shined the ones Dad had fixed that day. If that added up to enough for the picture show and if something good was on, Maria and I went. Otherwise we just walked around town, watching the farmers and townspeople milling on the streets.

That night we were in luck, each with two dimes, one for the show and one for popcorn.

I split my dessert, Fig Newtons, with Maria while we waited for show time. Drop-ins began to come in up front, *squeak, clack, squeak, clack*. Mother and Dad went to wait on them, if they were customers, or to visit, if they had just come to socialize.

A curtain separated the back room from the front. Maria and I peeked through it when we heard a ruckus. A small crowd had gathered in the store.

Two young men left shoes to be half-soled. They went out just as Kuppa Coffey came in, his newspaper bag still slung over his shoulder and an old pair of shoes in one hand.

A man I didn't recognize glared after the two as the door swung shut. " 'Tisn't right, young able-bodied men like that deferred when other boys are over there fighting," he said.

"Hold on there, bud," said another man. "You don't know they're able-bodied. Could be four-F, physically unfit, for some reason that doesn't show—bad eyes, poor hearing, ailing heart."

"Those country boys aren't ailing. They just don't want to go to war," the stranger said.

"Government needs those farm boys right where they are," the other one insisted. "Who do you think's going to feed our boys over there, the Nazis?"

Dad frowned from behind the counter. He didn't like arguments, especially in his store. He raised his hand to quiet them, but Kuppa spoke up first.

"Leave them alone, will you, mister?" he said to the stranger. "I play ball with those guys' brothers. I know their dads. They're all good folks."

"Well, it seems like someone else could do the farming," the man grumbled.

Mother stepped forward and spoke gently. "Are you volunteering, sir? What a gracious, patriotic thing to do." There was not a hint of teasing in her voice, and she held his gaze.

Someone stifled a guffaw. Silence fell over the store. The man touched the tip of his cap, nodded slightly to Mother, and stepped out into the evening.

Kuppa broke the silence. "Besides," he said as he handed his shoes to Dad, "when I get over there, we won't need anybody else."

Everyone laughed. Someone slapped Kuppa's back, and the chatter started up again. Adults in a shoe store sounded a lot like kids in a garden, I thought. I stepped through the curtains when I heard the name *Rommel*. Maria followed. What about Rommel, the infamous German general?

I elbowed in on a group gathered at the counter

around the Kansas City newspaper and leaned in to see the headline: "Tunisian War Ends."

One man read, " 'Six months after the Allied landings in North Africa, the Battle of Tunisia has come to a happy end. Field Marshal Erwin Rommel, the "Desert Fox," has fled to Europe. For the second time in World War II, a great German army has crumpled.' "

A whoop went up.

"That's here," I said. I had moved to the wall map Dad had pieced together from the free ones he got at the filling station. The men turned to see where I was pointing.

"You knew that?" one of the men asked.

"She knows maps," Maria said, throwing me a grin.

We danced off to see Fred Astaire, working our way around all the folks catching up on the week's news. Gossip mingled with talk of the war. The end still seemed far away. But beating Rommel! Surely that put it close.

CHAPTER 9

I should have slept like the dead, but I lay awake, my mind rattling inside my brain. The movie had only temporarily erased the garden. I saw peppers, beans and cucumbers behind eyelids that wouldn't stay closed. In a week all those vegetables would be ready to sell.

Tomatoes, on the other hand, would be a long time coming. Their tiny beginnings still lazed in the drying petals, and each day brought a new sprinkling of yellow blossoms. The same in Dad's garden. What about the secret weapon? Did I have to keep that a secret now that I had my own—well, Mr. Burt's—tomatoes? I'd sleep on it, as Mother would say. By morning something might come to me.

In fact, it didn't take that long.

I turned to the open window, curled up and let the

breeze touch my face. Outside, a sliver of moon chalked a perfect C on a blackboard sky. A streetlight etched a pale rim around the Burts' garden, but Saint Francis stood in the dark.

In the dark! Holding my eyes open, I lay still and listened. When I could hear nothing but the crickets, I got up, groped for my overalls and pulled them on. I held my shoes in one hand and opened the door just far enough to squeeze through, then shut it behind me. I tiptoed past my parents' closed door and down the stairs, skipping the steps I usually landed on hard just to hear them creak.

With a flashlight I grabbed from the workroom, I made my way safely out the back door. I dropped my shoes onto the soft grass, worked my bare feet into them and drew in a breath of night air. This was the right thing to do. I had promised not to tell the secret. I hadn't promised not to use it!

I picked my way across the street to a row of the Burts' tomatoes. Then I turned on the flashlight and held it close to the plants, keeping the circle of light as small as possible.

I worked quickly as sleepiness took hold. In the morning I scarcely remembered getting back across the street and upstairs to bed.

On Sundays we slept late, ate a long, slow breakfast, and still had time to dress for church. I loved Sundays— except for the one when Tom Burt had gotten hurt, of course. I shuddered, recalling Mrs. Burt's frantic call. This time it was a knock at the door just as I bit into my one strip of Sunday-only bacon.

"I'll get it," Dad said. I followed him into the living room.

"Morning, Alan," I heard someone say.

"Why, Hank, what brings you out so early on a Sunday morning? Come in, come in."

I grasped the back of the rocking chair. A shiny badge on his pocket was all that identified Hank Bonner as an officer of the law, but everybody knew he was the county sheriff. Sheriff Hank wore his official uniform at public affairs, but most days his uniform was the plaid shirt he wore that morning.

"Howdy, Teresa," said the sheriff.

"Have you found Old Wolf?" I asked, desperately hoping that was it.

"No, I'm sorry, little lady. No sign of the dog."

"Can we help you, Sheriff?" said Dad.

"Wondered if you saw anything unusual going on over at the Burts' last night."

I looked away.

"I don't think so," said Dad. "Why?"

"We had a complaint. Lady thought she saw a light moving around over there in the night."

I leaned over the chair and fluffed a ruffled pillow, hoping the beating in my chest was not as loud to their ears as to mine.

"Mrs. Greer, no doubt. The poor woman complains of insomnia."

"Can't say who. Rules, you know. Sure you didn't see anything?"

"I'm sure. Teresa?"

I jumped at my name.

"You were closer. Did you see anything unusual from your window?"

"No." That was true. Not from my window.

"What's happened, Sheriff?" asked Dad.

"Well, come have a look."

I trailed them across the street, torn between the need to know and the dread of finding out.

What I saw made me gasp. A ragged path of trampled plants led from one corner of the garden to the sandstone slab. Mrs. Burt's statue lay broken into chunks, one at the base of the pedestal, one upside down in the plants. The hand of Saint Francis, still holding the bird, lay almost hidden beneath a trampled vine.

Tears stung my eyes. Dad's arm folded around my shoulder.

"The kids worked here yesterday, but they aren't the culprits. I came by after work and everything was fine then. Poor Tom."

I noticed that he used only Mr. Burt's first name.

Poor Tom's wife, I thought. Tiny Mrs. Burt, holding her husband's hand in the ambulance. Mischievous Mrs. Burt, slipping warm cookies to me before dinnertime. Kind Mrs. Burt, sowing love everywhere, like Saint Francis. It was her statue, after all. But Dad had his own thoughts. "As if the tractor accident wasn't enough," he said. "Then Old Wolf disappears, and now this."

The sheriff nodded. "Well, Tom's a tough old bird. He'll survive his injuries better than losing his dog." He picked up the statue's hand. "This won't make him any happier."

"Surely we'll find the dog, Sheriff. No one has had the heart to tell the Burts yet."

"Yeah, I should think. Dogs wander off and eventually come home."

I hoped it was so, but Old Wolf had not wandered off from his home. He had run away from a place that was strange to him, miles and miles from here.

"No need to worry the Burts about the dog, then, or about this, either." Dad knelt beside the toppled statue. "We can fix it. The breaks are clean. Strong glue and careful matching should do it."

The men stood up and looked around at the plants. "They're not so bad, either," the sheriff said. "Leaves knocked off, but no damage to the roots."

"Who would do this?" Dad wondered aloud.

The sheriff shook his head. "Hard to tell. And it sprinkled just enough in the night to wash away telltale footprints."

"Teresa," Dad said, his voice jolting me, "did you see anything in the garden last night? Anything at all? Think hard."

While I hesitated, the sheriff bent over one of the crumpled tomato plants. "Uh-oh," he said, pulling something from among the leaves. "We may have a clue here."

Eagerly I looked to see what he had. My eyes widened. Dad coughed. The sheriff held a blue striped baseball cap. I looked from the sheriff to Dad and back. The sheriff held the cap out for Dad to see, eyeing him curiously. For what seemed like a very long while, no one said a word.

Finally Dad spoke. "This could have been dropped at any time."

The sheriff stood with feet spread apart, arms folded over his chest. Without taking his eyes off Dad, he said, "Yes. I s'pose you could have missed it when you had your look around."

My throat felt raw and my eyes stung, but I held out my hand for the cap. I ran my finger over the crooked red *T* I had so proudly embroidered over the bill. "This is mine, Sheriff Hank," I said. I looked around at the broken statue and torn plants and whispered, "But I didn't do this."

Dad's hand was firm on my back, his fingers pressing hard between my shoulder blades. "We'll keep an eye out tonight, Sheriff, and let you know if we see anything," he said.

"Fine."

The sheriff gave Saint Francis's hand, with the bird, to me, then lifted one chunk of the statue for Dad to carry and reached for the other piece. "Oh-oh," he said again as he turned it over. He touched a finger to the jagged edge. "This looks like blood."

I closed my eyes and held the statue's hand close to my chest. Tears pushed out from under my lids.

"I'd best keep the statue in custody for a few days," the sheriff said. "It's evidence." He held out his hand. "Afraid I'll have to keep the cap, too. Sorry."

The walk back across the street was a long journey. Dad was silent until we were seated on the front steps.

"There must be some explanation, Teresa. Your cap

was on the kitchen counter when I went in for supper last night. And I think Mother reminded you to put it away."

"She did." I had rolled it up and stuck it in my back overall pocket, which was where I kept it. It must have fallen out as I worked in the darkened garden.

"What's going on, Teresa?"

"Dad, I didn't do anything to Mr. Burt's statue. Or tramp on his plants."

"But you know who did?"

"Billy Riggs, that's who!" I said. "I'll just bet."

He glanced at my bare head. "Be careful about accusing people, Teresa. Even when you think you have evidence. Were you there?"

"Not when the statue got broken."

"But sometime?"

" 'Fraid so."

"When?"

"I'm not sure, exactly. It was after everybody was in bed."

"Teresa!" He stood up, folded his arms and eyed me like the sheriff had eyed him. "Haven't we ever told you that you can't go out in the middle of the night by yourself?"

"I don't think so."

"But a smart girl like you would know that, wouldn't she?"

"I wasn't afraid," I said. "I went to use the secret weapon."

"You *what*?"

"I didn't tell anyone the secret, Dad. I just used it. Mr. Burt won't know, even if we win. I didn't think you'd be mad."

He nearly exploded. "Young lady, you are missing the point. You went out in the night without permission. If someone else was prowling in the garden, you put yourself in danger. That's not fair to your mother and me."

Especially when Jeff is in danger already. He might as well have said it. I barely managed, "I'm sorry."

"All right." He sat down again, tugging his trouser legs up as he did. "I'm going to let it pass—this time. We'd better get dressed for church."

As we stood to go in, he reached for my hand. "About the tomatoes," he said. "It's just a contest. It's just for fun."

"I know," I said. But we both knew it was more than that.

CHAPTER 10

$\mathcal{I}$n church, I fingered the lace on my dress while the preacher talked about forgiveness. Funny he should bring that up right then. I thought about my midnight escapade. I thought about the words on the statue: *Where there is injury, pardon.* And I thought a lot about Billy Riggs.

Dad stayed after church to meet with the deacons. At home I changed into overalls and set the table for Sunday dinner. Mother and I hummed in the kitchen, the closing hymn still in our ears.

I peeled the potatoes, struggling to make the peelings as thin as possible. Mother smiled her approval. Later, she would drain them, add fresh water and put them on the stove to boil, while her chicken sizzled in a frying pan. Dad would mash them into a mound of white fluff just before we sat down to eat.

My part of the chores done, I strolled across to pick some of Mrs. Burt's flowers. Colors burst beside the walks. Petunias, purple, red and white, edged the yard. Against the white latticework of the porch, Mrs. Burt's showy peonies bore giant blossoms of pink and lavender. How she must miss them!

The last bright yellow tulip bowed on its stem. I stooped to snap it. Sounds came from behind the Burts' house, faint, high-pitched whimpers. Curious, I walked to the backyard and peered into the dark space under the porch. This had been my old hideaway a long time ago, before the war, before the gardens. I'd almost forgotten it.

The Burts had moved in from the country right after my sixth birthday. Mother made a welcome cake and a pitcher of tea. While she and Mrs. Burt sat talking in the kitchen, sipping the tea, I slipped out through the screen door and down the steps. I saw a gap in the lattice around the back porch. Out of orneriness, I crawled inside and hid. I curled up in the cool dirt and fell asleep.

When I stirred, I thought elephants were stomping on the porch above me. Adult voices drowned each other out. Legs showed through the lattice, hurrying back and forth. Someone yelled, "I found her!" and Jeff's head appeared, upside down, in the open space I had crawled through. I was fine then, but I felt like crying now as I remembered Jeff saying, "You're in trouble, squirt."

It was worth it. I had discovered the perfect place to sit with my dolls on days too hot for roller skating. I spent most of that summer under the porch. I must have been really small then.

I couldn't see anything under there now. I turned to go, but the whimpers came again, and something else.

"Shhh, shhh."

I dropped to my hands and knees and squinted. "Who's here?"

A rasping whisper answered me. "Get out!"

I shuddered, but my curiosity won out. I flattened myself against the ground and inched forward on my elbows.

"Who are you?" I whispered, since he had whispered.

"None of your beeswax!" He shouted it this time.

"Billy Riggs!" I shouted back. "I knew it!"

"Knew what?"

"You broke Mr. Burt's statue!"

"Get out."

A pitiful yelp interrupted us. I squinted to see better and elbowed further in. A scraggly black animal stared at me through narrowed yellow eyes.

"Is that a dog?"

"None of your business, I told ya."

"It sounds hurt."

"Well, no kidding. I just about had him settled down till you came bargin' in. Now get out."

"What's the matter with him?"

"He's hurt, dummy. Said so yourself."

"Hurt where?" I scooted further in. Billy was scrunched up beside the animal.

"His back leg's all cut up, maybe broke."

"Oh, my golly! How'd he get in here?"

"Limped in. Found him in the alley, 'fore sunup."

"You've been here all that time? Won't your folks be worried?"

"Huh!" he said. "Dog was in awful shape. Bleedin'. Near starved."

"What did you do?"

"Tried to help. He just cried and shied away. I followed him here."

"Oh, my golly," I said again.

He seemed to forget that he wanted me out, and started telling me more. "I ran home for some old rags. Brought this old coffee can for water. All's I could do was rinse off his leg and wrap some rags around it."

"I could get him some food," I said.

"No need. I stole some hamburger from the icebox. Dogs can eat raw meat, can't they?"

Stole? "Why didn't you just ask your mom?"

"Huh!"

The day before, I couldn't have imagined Billy being kind to anything, let alone a stray animal. I'd have thought he'd throw rocks at it. "Why are you doing this?" I asked him.

"He ain't done nothin'. Just got hurt, that's all."

"Are you going to take him home with you?"

"Huh!" It came out like a bullet. "My old man would kick him down the well."

Maybe there was a reason why Billy was so mean.

The animal whined.

"I'll get my mother," I said. "She knows Red Cross first aid. Wait here."

"Well, now, where would I be goin'?" He sounded more relieved than defiant.

Mother and I hurried back, carrying a first-aid kit and a flattened pasteboard box, Mother's idea. Billy eased the dog onto the pasteboard, and we pulled it out from under the porch. Billy elbowed his way out, blinking against the sunlight.

When we saw the dog, we gasped.

It was not a medium-sized black dog, like I'd thought. This was a large animal, tall and long, but so skinny and matted that he had looked small when he lay in a heap under the porch. In the light I could see patches of yellow-brown fur through the mud and tar.

"Wolfie?" I said, not quite believing. "It is! It's him!" I flung my arms around Old Wolf's neck.

"Hey, don't hurt him!" Billy said. He stroked the dog's ear. "We gotta get you well, dog."

I had never heard this kind of tone from Billy Riggs.

Mother knelt. "Can you two hold him still while I examine his leg?" I held Wolfie's head, and Billy put both arms over his rear. Mother probed the leg gently. "I don't think it's broken, but it is badly cut. A deep gash on the foot. Teresa, hand me the Mercurochrome."

I rummaged through the kit and pulled out a small bottle of red liquid. When my mother treated my cuts, she painted the medicine on with the thin glass wand attached to the cap. For Old Wolf, she poured it into the large wounds. He yelped but lay still and looked at us with wide eyes. Maybe he knew we were helping him.

Mother wrapped his leg with a clean strip of white

rag, split the last few inches of the cloth, and tied the two ends.

"We should wash him off with the hose," Billy said. "Cool him down a little."

"Good idea," Mother said. "Bring him over to our house."

Billy knelt on the grass and stretched his arms out in front of him. "Put him here," he said.

Mother and I followed Billy's instructions without questioning. I took one end of the pasteboard, Mother took the other, and we lifted it, dog and all, onto Billy's outstretched arms.

"Are you sure he's not too heavy?" we asked.

"Nah. He ain't but skin and bones."

We followed behind as the meanest kid in town carried an ailing dog, like a baby in a cradle, across the street. Mother said, "If you two can manage the dog, I'll go put the chicken on to cook. Would you like to eat with us, Billy?"

I just about died. I was impressed with Billy's care of the dog, but have him to dinner? What if the kids found out?

We ran a few inches of water into Mother's washtub and lifted Old Wolf into it. Billy gripped him by the loose skin behind his head while I held the hose. The cool water softened and rinsed away the crusts of mud. We couldn't do much about the tar.

Dad came up just as we were patting Old Wolf dry.

"Dad, look! It's Old Wolf! We found him," I called when he was barely out of the car.

Billy cleared his throat.

"I mean, Billy found him."

Dad hurried up the walk and bent over the dog. "Well, I'll be," he said, kneading the top of Wolf's head with his knuckles.

Billy and I both talked at once, spilling out the story.

"The sheriff was right, then," Dad said.

"What?" Billy jerked, causing Old Wolf to yelp. For an instant he looked . . . I don't know, panicked, I guess. Then he went all casual. " 'Bout what?"

"He said dogs find their way home, but I'd never known it to be from so far away."

"Oh."

I hadn't thought to introduce Billy properly. Dad extended his hand. "Good work. Billy, is it? I'm Alan Marks."

Billy put his hand out, looking awkward. "Billy Riggs."

I saw Dad's eyebrow lift.

"We'll ask Mother for a blanket," he said to me. "We can bed the dog down in the workroom."

We urged Old Wolf to the back door. He loped on three legs, even up the steps. In the workroom off the kitchen, he sank onto the thick cotton comforter Mother had already spread for him. We watched as he lapsed into sleep.

The smell of frying chicken wafted in from the kitchen. I realized I was famished. Billy must have felt as starved as Old Wolf. He had fed the dog, but I'd have bet he hadn't had anything himself since breakfast. If he'd had that.

In spite of myself, I took his arm and led him into the kitchen. I didn't wait for him to protest.

Mother was spearing golden brown chicken pieces with a two-pronged fork and lifting them out of the hot skillet. She piled them on an oval platter.

"You two can wash up at the sink. I'm glad you've decided to stay, Billy."

Billy had decided no such thing. "I can't. My folks will be expecting me."

I knew that was not true. But tough Billy Riggs had suddenly turned shy.

Mother sensed his discomfort.

"Well, at least take some chicken home with you." When Billy looked doubtful, she insisted. "A whole chicken is much too much for the three of us."

Billy stuck his hands in his pockets. He smiled with one side of his mouth and said, "Well, ma'am, I reckon it would be hard to kill half a chicken."

I watched him eye the chicken hungrily as my mother transferred a drumstick from the platter to a small plate. I noted with mixed guilt and gratitude that the three pieces she put on the plate did not include the wishbone.

But I formed a wordless O when she pulled a length of waxed paper from the box, snapped it across the serrated edge, and laid it over the oval platter. She topped that with the red-and-white checked dish towel she reserved for church supper casseroles, and handed the whole thing to Billy!

"You'll be coming back to see Wolf, I'm sure. You can bring the platter back then."

Billy's eyes were wide. "Yes, ma'am. Thank you."

He backed out of the kitchen, both hands occupied with the platter, pushed the screen door open with one elbow, and was gone.

Mother lifted the lid off a steaming pot and tested the potatoes with the long fork, humming as she worked. I looked at the small plate holding one chicken leg, one thigh and one wing, and then at Dad. He lifted a shoulder and said, "We can have an extra slice of bread if we're still hungry."

CHAPTER 11

I raced upstairs after school the next day, slid the top dresser drawer out and felt around for my old hairbrush. There it was in the back, where I had shoved it after finding a new one in my Christmas stocking.

Old Wolf lay sleeping when I pushed open the door off the kitchen a few minutes later. His sides pulsed in even breaths. As I tiptoed toward him, he stirred, raised his head and followed me with wary eyes.

"It's okay, Wolfie," I said, kneeling beside him. I stroked his neck with my brush. He whimpered at first but soon closed his eyes, lulled by the rhythmic strokes.

As I brushed him I thought again about Billy. What made him care so much about a hurt, battered dog?

"What do you think, Wolfie?" I asked him as I pulled

the brush through his now clean fur. "Maybe Billy had finally found a friend in you. Then we came along and took you away from him."

That might explain Billy's unusual behavior at school that day, or rather his usual behavior.

What had I expected? That Billy had been transformed into a good guy by one kind deed to a dog? I had thought I'd go up to him and tell him how Wolfie was doing. But I couldn't. The playground teacher was pulling him by the arm toward the principal's office when I got there. He had been in one of his fistfights, this time with some upper-grade kids. When he got to class, red-faced and angry, he'd already missed half of reading. He stared out the window the rest of the day.

Old Wolf let out soft moans of contentment as I stroked and talked. "I can't figure Billy out, Wolfie," I said. "I admit I'm glad I didn't have to talk to him." I didn't relish being teased for huddling with the most hated pupil in school, a boy at that. But I was sure Billy had a good streak as well as a bad one. So why hadn't I told Miss Elliott or someone about his good deed?

"Nobody would have believed me," I said, more to myself than to the dog. "Not the way he was acting today." I pulled the brush over Old Wolf's side in a deep, massaging stroke. He jerked, then growled, and snapped at me.

"Wolfie!" I sat back on my heels and ran my fingers cautiously along his side. Something sharp, like a small, jagged rock, pricked my finger. Parting the fur, I saw a chunk of something stuck in the flesh.

"Easy, boy. We can get that out." I reached for the Red Cross kit and took out a long, tweezer-like instrument I had seen Mother use. Lying with one arm over the dog's body to steady him, I eased the pincers around the chunk. When I had it just right, I gripped the end of the pincers and slowly pulled it out. It left a small, bleeding wound. The dog yelped.

"It's okay, Wolfie." I opened the Mercurochrome bottle, now nearly empty, and poured the remaining medicine into the wound. One more yelp and Old Wolf settled into the comforter. I picked up the pincers, intending to return them to the box. They still held the thing I had pulled from the dog's side. I held it up for a closer look.

"Oh, my golly!" I whispered.

I stroked Wolfie's head and smoothed out the comforter. "Good dog. Good old boy," I said. "I have to leave, but I'll be right back." I looked at the clock. Five minutes. If I hurried, I could make it before closing time.

I wrapped the pincers and the chunk in waxed paper, which, I reasoned, would not soak up or dry out the fresh blood. Then I grabbed a paper sack, put the parcel into it and rushed out.

The sheriff's office was three blocks away, on the second floor of the courthouse. I sprinted the last half block and pushed open the heavy double doors as workers poured down the long curved staircase. I dashed up past them and caught Sheriff Hank just as he was locking his door.

"Sheriff," I gasped, out of breath.

"Ho, where to, little lady?"

"I have something to tell you!"

"It must be mighty important."

"It is. Old Wolf came home."

"The Burts' dog?"

"Yes. Billy Riggs found him in the alley behind their house. He—"

"Slow down." The sheriff looked hard at me. His eyebrows pulled together. "Riggs, you say? When?"

"Sunday morning."

"Yesterday?"

"Yes. Old Wolf found his way home, just like you said he would."

"I'm glad to hear that, Teresa. Thanks for telling me." He put his keys in his pocket and gave the door a try to be sure it was locked.

I talked even faster, afraid he would start moving down the long hall toward the stairs. "Wolf was all cut up when Billy found him, especially his foot. We thought a car had hit him. My mother dressed his wounds, and Billy and I gave him a hose bath."

"Good. That's one case closed, then. The case of the missing dog." He jingled the keys in his pocket, the way grown-ups do when they want to get going.

"But there's more!" I stuck the sack out. "I have evidence! Please! You've got to look!"

"Well . . ." He pulled the keys out. "We'd better step inside."

I set the sack on his desk and unwound the waxed paper.

"See what it is?" I said.

"Hmm." The sheriff held up the pincers. "I think so."

"See what's on it? It's blood."

"Well, yes. But whose blood?"

"Old Wolf's."

I was sure he looked relieved. "Well, I'll be," he said. "You pulled this out? That was pretty brave. You're a gardener and a veterinarian, too."

I liked both names better than "little lady." "Thank you," I said.

"The dog must have been excited to see home but frustrated that the Burts weren't there," the sheriff speculated. "He probably ran back and forth across the garden—"

"And that would have messed up the plants," I said.

"My guess is he recognized the statue and jumped up on it."

"Like he would have jumped up on Mr. Burt if he'd been there?"

The sheriff nodded. "The statue must have fallen on him. Either that or he just came crashing down with it."

I put my thumbnail between my teeth. "Maybe," I said.

"Looks like the statue case is closed, too, then. Good work, little la—little gardener, animal doctor and detective."

He could have left out the "little," but I liked the rest of it. "Thank you, Sheriff," I said.

He put the pincers, chunk and all, back into the sack and handed it to me. "Tell your father he can pick up the statue anytime. I know he wants to mend it before the Burts come home."

"I will," I said, and turned to leave.

"Just a minute," the sheriff said. "I have something you want, I'm sure." He opened a desk drawer. "I won't need this anymore."

Tears stung my lids as he held out my blue striped cap. I could barely whisper a thank-you.

"It didn't fit me," he said, changing my tears to giggles.

Hurrying back home to Old Wolf, I wondered if a dog, even a big dog could really knock a statue down.

CHAPTER 12

$\mathcal{E}$llie was first with something to sell. Her uncle, true to his word, bought the early radishes and paid her an astonishing fifty cents. "Bonus for the first things from the garden," he said.

Getting rid of the peppers was not so easy. Maria and I went door to door with Ellie after school, since we had no tomatoes or peas to sell yet.

Her neighbors admired the peppers, green and shining in a wicker basket, but no one needed them. "Let me give you some of mine," one said. "We planted way too many!"

"What if everybody planted too many?" said Maria as we turned away.

Or too much of everything, I thought, but I said, "Let's guess who might say yes."

The late-afternoon sun blazed orange as we reached Theda Buell's front walk with one last pepper.

"I guess no." We all spoke at once and giggled. Theda Buell, living by herself at the far corner of town, had no children and no use for them.

I grinned. "Want to bet I can do it?"

"Bet, but no money," said Ellie.

A long pause followed our knock. The door opened a few inches.

"Ye-es?" The woman's voice rose at the end of the word. Her mouth made a straight line, and her lips barely parted.

I felt my grin fade, and I swallowed. "Good afternoon, Miss Buell."

"Ye-es?"

"I . . . we . . ." I started again. "We are selling peppers from Mr. Tom Burt's garden, and we have only one left."

"Ye-es?"

"Would you like to buy it?"

The woman said nothing.

"Uh, it's three cents, Miss Buell. Would you like it?"

"No-o. Don't like peppers."

The door closed while my mouth was still open.

We turned back down the walk. "What makes people—" I began.

Ellie broke in, singing.

> *"What makes a lady of eighty*
> *Go out on the loose?"*

Maria picked it up.

> *"Why does the gander meander*
> *In search of a goose?"*

And we finished together.

> *"What puts the kick in*
> *The chicken, the magic in June?"*

By then we were shouting.

> *"It's just Elmer's tune!"*

We bumped rumps, giggled, and kept on walking. "I should've bet money," said Ellie.

My mind drifted. The month of May had tiptoed right into June and we'd scarcely noticed. Before we knew it we had finished our readers, used up the last paper from our tablets and wondered aloud if we'd passed. But that next-to-last day of school seemed longer than the whole year leading up to it.

I shifted in my seat and pictured what the last day would be like. We would forget about lessons and work and war. We'd run relay races, play ball and eat the enormous picnic dinner our mothers would spread out on tables.

Everyone seemed restless today. Billy Riggs was out of his seat more than in it. He broke the tip off his lead pencil and darted to the sharpener. Now's my chance, I thought. I raised the top of my desk just far enough to reach in for an unsharpened pencil of my own. Standing behind Billy, I looked out the open window. No air moved. Branches of the one schoolyard tree hung limp, as if painted on the sky.

I tapped Billy on the shoulder, but he wouldn't turn around. Why was he acting this way? Why hadn't he come back to see Old Wolf? He could have brought the platter back as an excuse, and besides, Mother had invited him. He cranked the sharpener's handle and bolted to his seat.

I thought back to the day he'd found Old Wolf. Billy had jumped a mile when Dad suggested telling the sheriff. And hadn't the sheriff looked at me oddly just a few days ago when I'd mentioned Billy's name?

Ellie was adamant. "I won't do it!" she said, her lips barely parting over clenched teeth. "There is no way I'm going to tie my leg to his!" The relays were about to begin, and Ellie was stuck with Billy Riggs in the three-legged race.

We had eaten until we ached. Not even food rationing put a crimp in the last-day-of-school picnic. Chickens raised at home didn't require ration coupons; we gobbled drumsticks and tangy deviled eggs. Gardens provided for potato salad, red pickled beets and home-canned green beans with slivers of bacon.

The strawberry Jell-O with bananas didn't even count as dessert. That was apple pie or peanut butter cookies or chocolate cake piled high with frosting, all made with precious sugar saved from rations for this special day.

"I'll trade places with you in the race," I told Ellie. I

wanted to know what was going on with Billy. He had avoided me all day, not that I'd tried very hard to be with him in front of all these people. He was, as always, the last to be chosen for any of the games or races. I had always thought that was because he was unpopular, but maybe he was unpopular because he wasn't good at games.

I looked across at him now and realized how small he was. He'd just always seemed bigger. He might be slow on his feet, but he was quick with his hands and quicker with his temper. I felt a little sorry for him in spite of how exasperating he could be and in spite of my suspicions.

I let him tie my left foot to his right one. I looked down at his head as he worked an old scarf into a knot just above our ankles. His hair looked like a haystack caught in a mudslide. Some of the mud must have dried behind his ears.

I said, "Old Wolf is doing fine."

Billy grunted. "His foot okay?"

"Much better. You did a great job with him."

"Yeah." Billy concentrated on the tying.

"You won't believe what I found."

Billy's hands stopped for a moment. "What?"

"A sharp chunk from the statue stuck into his side. I pulled it out. It was all bloody."

His hands stopped again for a split second. "I didn't know. . . ." He kept his eyes on our ankles.

I caught his hesitation but said only, "Hurry up. The others are ready."

We came in last, of course. The heel of Billy's shoe had come loose and was just hanging; that might have been part of it. We untied ankles, and he melted into a swarm of kids and adults. I probably wouldn't see him again until school started in the fall.

CHAPTER 13

The Sprouts declared a day off as soon as vacation began. I stayed in bed as long as I could, finished my library book in the mulberry tree and clamped on my roller skates. Skating was as close as I could come to flying.

I spread my arms for wings and pretended I was soaring over some foreign country, winning the war with Jeff. We had women pilots, I knew, called WASPs, for Women Airforce Service Pilots. They were important to the war and to Jeff. They delivered the B24s to the pilots overseas, but they couldn't go into battle. I didn't see why not.

I banked to the right and was abruptly grounded. A wheel came whirling off my skate, and I crash-landed right in Mrs. Burt's petunias. Except for smashed blossoms and one skinned elbow, it was a non-injury crash. I found the wheel and put it in my pocket, took off the skates and buckled the ankle straps together, then slung them over my shoulder. As long as I was there, I'd inspect Mr. Burt's garden, day off or not.

I bent to finger a green tomato, round and hard still, but now big as a shooting marble. It would swell to full size, ripe and juicy, in a matter of weeks. Water made that happen! The plant was a pump, Mr. Burt had once told us. It pulled water up from the ground and into the tomatoes.

I dug my fingers into the dirt around the plants. It was still damp. No need to water that day.

The tomatoes might be small, but the peppers were bigger than my fist, the beans and pea pods as long as my hand. I flung my arms out and twirled around, skates knocking my chest and back. "It's working," I whispered into the air. "The garden is working!" I headed for home and my stationery drawer. I couldn't wait to tell Jeff.

By Saturday it seemed as if school had been out forever, not just three days. I was getting the willies. Would the Sprouts remember to come now that it was summer? Maybe I had rushed into this, gone off on my own one too many times. But I'd had to, hadn't I? To keep the garden from being plowed under?

In spite of our lavish school picnic in Shady Grove,

food was growing more scarce across America. I had cut a page from *Life* and saved it for the Young Sprouts. "Listen to this," I would say to them: "'Farm and Food Crisis! This year, the United States must produce more food than ever before.'" The picture showed an old grandfather and two little boys helping out on a farm. If they could do it, we could do it! I folded the page and put it in my pocket.

I laughed when Andy, of all people, showed up first.

"Hey, lazybones," he called through the screen door.

He should talk! But I grinned, seeing his freckled face.

They all came, as bored already with summer as I was. We got the hoes and trowels from behind my house and headed across the street. It felt right to be together again.

I watched the other kids as I worked. Some were fast and some were slow, but everybody did something. Not bad.

The talk turned to the end of school and Billy Riggs's fights.

"I heard a teacher say if they could keep Billy's hands tied behind him he wouldn't be so much trouble," said Maria.

"My dad said old man Riggs is a drunk," said Andy. "Said Billy won't amount to much."

"Your dad told you that?" said Ellie.

"Told my mom, but I heard him. Told me if I fight him, don't whine about a bloody nose." He rubbed his nose as he said it.

"He can't help who his father is," I said, scratching the ground with my hoe. "Billy could have a good side, too."

That brought a burst of protests.

"Who says? I've never seen a good side."

"I don't want to see *any* side."

"I hope he doesn't show up here again."

I wanted to agree, but I couldn't. I told them, finally, about Billy and Old Wolf, how Billy had stayed with the dog and tried to help him. "Look, Billy doesn't even like Mr. Burt, but he took care of the Burts' dog as if it was his own," I said. "That's his good side. I've seen it."

The others fell silent.

"I don't care," said Ellie in a quiet voice. "I hope he stays away from here."

In a way, I hoped so, too. I hadn't told them everything I knew, or thought I knew, about Billy Riggs.

The air was sticky, and our shirts clung to our backs. When the noon whistle called the town to its midday break, we took long drinks from the hose and squirted cold water on each other, squealing. We sprawled in the shade and attacked our sack lunches. While we ate, mostly from each other's sacks, we guessed at the money we would make.

"A bundle," said Andy, chomping on a carrot. He pointed the carrot at the garden. "Soon be loads of stuff to pick."

"But the money isn't really ours, is it?" said Maria. "I mean, except for savings stamps."

"Sure it is, if we earn it," said Andy. "Nobody said we had to spend everything on stamps."

"But didn't we say it was for stamps?"

They all looked at me. "What exactly did Mr. Burt say?"

I smiled. "All he said was that we had to win the *Chronicle*'s Great Tomato Duel."

"Yay!" they cheered. I wasn't sure whether it was for the tomatoes or the money.

"Poor Louise. Bet she's sorry she quit," said Ellie. "Did you see her face when all the kids came up to us after we got our names in the paper?"

Rich had been quiet. "Speaking of quitting . . ."

"You wouldn't! We're just getting started."

"I have to. My granddad's taken sick. They need me at the farm."

I folded my arms and gripped my own elbows. Rich did know his gardening. He didn't think of it as work, even though he'd said it was a long way from planting to picking. He saw my panic.

"You'll be fine," he said. "Granddad says nature does most of it, so don't go crazy."

Andy was watching a ladybug on his finger. "Sorry about your granddad," he said, breaking a nervous silence. He stuck the ladybug under Ellie's nose.

"Get that out of here!"

"Andy, cut it out," said Scott. He held Andy's wrist and moved it away from Ellie's face. "We'd better talk about how we're going to make all this money."

"Easy," said Andy. "Pick. Sell. Before the stuff rots."

"How do we know people will want it?" said Scott.

I had done plenty of worrying about that. With food

ripening in victory gardens all over town, who would need ours? But I argued for the bright side. "They'll need extra for canning."

Scott persisted. "Don't forget the competition."

"You think too much, Scott," said Andy. "What competition?"

"From the farmers. They'll soon be bringing vegetables to town to trade, along with their eggs and milk."

"I thought farm crops went overseas," said Ellie.

"The wheat, yes. But the vegetables that go over there come from huge commercial farms, not from the farms around here. When our farmers have extra produce, they bring it to town to sell. Every Saturday."

"So we beat them to it! Pick on Fridays, sell to the folks in town and carry it right to their doors. Save them walking to the store," said Andy.

"Why not just sell ours to the stores?" said Maria. "They could buy from us like they do from the farmers."

"Not likely," said Scott. "The farmers trade for other groceries. We want cash."

"We should run ads in the *Chronicle*," said Andy.

"Now who's thinking too much? Ads cost money," said Ellie.

"Not much if we keep it short," said Scott. "My mom ran an ad to sell a rocker; they charge three cents a word. Who has a pencil?"

"Me." Andy fished a stub out of a pocketful of junk.

We bickered over wording. Scott flattened his lunch sack and scribbled on it, scratched out and scribbled more. Finally he read back: " 'Young Sprouts Gardeners will be selling their vegetables door to door every Friday. Look for us!' "

He counted the words, then turned the sack over and worked the math on the back of the sack. "Forty-eight cents. Ouch!"

"Take out 'will be.' "

"And 'their.' "

Still too long.

"We don't need 'gardeners' and 'vegetables' both."

"Or 'every.' "

"Let's assume they'll look for us."

" 'Young Sprouts Gardeners selling door to door Fridays.' Twenty-four cents. There'll be five of us, without Rich. A nickel apiece and we draw straws to keep the extra penny."

I watched their faces. Except for Louise Lang, kids didn't have nickels jingling in their pockets. A nickel would buy an ice cream cone, double dip, or five B-B Bat suckers from Rexall Drugs. Come Harvest Festival, a nickel would get you a ride on the Ferris wheel.

I crossed my fingers for luck. "Let's see if we can charge the first ad and pay for it out of our first sales."

"I have to get home," said Ellie. "Are we done?"

"Done!" Andy gathered the top of his lunch sack, blew into the narrow opening, twisted it shut and popped it with his fist.

When I explained the plan to Dad later, he nodded. "You keep the Marks Bootery accounts, Mother," he said. "Can we underwrite that first ad? That way the Sprouts won't start out in debt."

Mother smiled. "I'll check the books," she said.

I hadn't mentioned Billy, but he was on my mind. What if he showed up to bother us again, or trampled the garden? He must have been on Mother's mind, too. "Where's your friend Billy?" she said. "He hasn't come back to see Old Wolf."

"He's not exactly my friend, Mother. Everybody hates him."

"Do you?"

"How can I, after what he did for Wolfie? I told the kids, but they don't want him around." I hunched my shoulders. "What can I do?"

Dad was the one who answered. "The boy may have a lot to overcome, but he's earned your respect. One day he may just earn theirs, too."

I doubted that. "All I know is, nobody's even seen him since the picnic. And nobody wants to."

CHAPTER 14

The familiar smell of leather and shoe polish greeted me like an old friend as I pushed open the Bootery door. As much as cookies baking or Mother's perfume, the smells in the shoe store meant home and comfort. I found Dad in the back room restacking the few remaining boxes of new shoes to make room for all the old ones waiting to be repaired. Mother was up front, working on her yellow ledger sheets.

From behind the curtain, I heard the front door open and Mother's voice saying, "Well, hello there."

I couldn't hear the soft reply, but Mother said, "Came clear off, did it? Well, have a seat. Perhaps we can fix it right now. Give me the other shoe and we'll make sure that heel doesn't come off, too. There are some magazines to look at while you wait."

I pulled the curtain open just at my eye level. Sure enough, here came Mother with Billy Riggs's shoes. Not only that. I heard her say, "We've been expecting to see you at the house, Billy."

I strained to hear him. "I keep forgettin' about that platter, ma'am." I wondered who had taught him to say *ma'am*.

"No, I mean to see Old Wolf."

Why couldn't we just leave things as they were?

Dad turned Billy's sad-sack shoe over in his hands and shook his head. I could see that reattaching the run-down heel to a sole that had a hole the size of Texas would not help much.

"Why don't you go out and visit with your friend?" Mother said.

"He's not my friend," I said between clenched teeth. But I went. Billy sat on the bench, trying to hide his feet under it. A big toe poked out through a hole in his sock.

"Hi," I said, standing behind the counter as though I owned the place.

"Hi." He kept his eyes on a magazine, turning pages too fast to read anything.

"Cat got your tongue?" I finally said.

"Got yours?"

Well, this was some visit.

Billy concentrated on a full-page aircraft company advertisement. I recognized the pictured airplane by the double tail. Not many planes had two rudders. "That's the best airplane there is," I said, forgetting myself and coming around the counter. "The B-twenty-four Liberator."

"It is not."

"Oh, no? What's better?" I knew the B-24. He didn't have anything on me just because he was a boy and drew war pictures all the time.

"B-seventeen, for one. The Flying Fortress. Now, that's a plane."

"This one goes faster," I said, poking my finger at the page.

"It's a box. Look at it. Clunky."

"And it goes farther," I said, ignoring him, "and carries more bombs than your precious Fortress."

"Looks like an elephant with ears on the wrong end. Besides, the seventeens do all the important stuff."

"They do not." I stomped over to Dad's map. Before I knew it, I was jabbing at the map like a schoolteacher, pointing to places B-24s had flown into battle, some on every front. I knew these places. I had pasted news clippings about them in the scrapbook I was making for Jeff.

"Midway Island, between Hawaii and Japan," I announced. "Obvious why we needed that, isn't it?" I moved back and forth across the map.

"Ploesti, where Hitler keeps his oil supply. He can't run his ships without oil, can he?

"The Aleutians, so the Japanese can't attack us from there." I kept going. "Solomon Islands, Wake—"

I must say, Billy showed more interest than Maria had. He was standing beside me now with his mouth open.

But all he said was "Strange map."

* * *

Summer came on its best behavior, saving us the trouble of holding the hose. Days were hot, but night rains cooled the gardens. I knew what Mrs. Burt would have said if she'd been there: No hand but God's could water a garden so well.

Still, the Young Sprouts were working hard. Nature had not found a way to pull weeds, pluck off bugs or pick the vegetables. If Mrs. Burt could have seen us, she'd have been proud.

The front door stood open as I straightened the living room one drizzly day. I pushed the carpet sweeper and breathed in the damp morning air. Outside, the rain fell fine as mist, slanting in under the roof to wet a strip of porch.

Was it raining where Jeff was? Was it morning or was it night?

"Remember when we rode in the rain, Jeff, me on the handlebars, you pedaling through the puddles? You said don't tell Mom." Sometimes I remembered him so well, I spoke out loud like that.

Other times I'd forget what he looked like. The picture I dusted every week didn't help. The uniform looked strange. The face, nearly covered by the bill of an officer's cap, was too old to be Jeff's. I tried to hear him calling me "squirt," but no sound came with the memory. Did I have a brother?

As if to answer my question, the postman rattled the screen door, his way of announcing that he'd pulled a letter from overseas out of his worn brown pouch. I dropped the handle of the sweeper and ran to the door.

"Morning, Teresa," he said through the screen. Raindrops dripped from his uniform cap.

"Oh, thank you, Mr. Lewis!" I said as I pushed the screen door open and reached for the mail.

Jeff's letter was on top. His letters often came in bunches, after a long stretch of none at all. Today there was only one. Yes! I whooped at the address on the envelope: *Miss Teresa Marks, Shady Grove, Kansas, USA.*

I sat in Dad's armchair, my feet dangling over one side.

Dear Teresa,

Whoa, you're full of questions! Thanks for your letter. I am lucky that you and the folks write. Some guys don't get mail at all.

Know you're busy, especially if you are tending Tom Burt's garden. Keep up the good work, 'cause what you do counts. That answers your first question. Of course it's up to Tom Burt and Dad, but I hope they didn't plow it under.

Second question. Yes, I guess you and Dad are the "duelers" now. Whose side is Mom on?

Your third question is hard to answer, what's it like to be flying "up there." It's noisy—bumpy— freezing cold even with our electric flying suits. But it makes me feel free, like I'm sledding over air. When I was a little kid I wanted to be Santa

Claus. Then I found out there were even better things to fly than sleighs!

Fourth, there isn't much time to be scared. What I do is more like work than fighting. We're up there for hours at a time. Boring, sometimes, but always busy. We have lunch out of a box and just keep on flying. What I wouldn't give for one of your tomatoes up there, squirt!

Love,
Jeff

P.S. By the way, exactly what is that secret weapon, and how does it work? You never told me.

I'd had a few days of peace without Billy. He still hadn't taken Mother up on her invitation. Dad had brought his shoes out from the Bootery's back room with brand-new heels, new half soles and polish that made them look as good as run-down shoes could look. Billy's mouth had dropped open, and a scared look had crossed his face. But he'd relaxed when Dad said, "On the house, for saving Old Wolf. You come see him, now."

I winced. Billy had found the dog; he hadn't exactly saved him. We'd all done that, and I had been the one to feed him and walk him once his leg was healed. We couldn't send him away again after he had come all that way to get home to the Burts.

We had just started out one morning, earlier than usual, when Old Wolf began to whine and strain at the leash. I pulled back, but he stripped the leash out of my hand and went darting across the street, right into the arms of you-know-who.

"Hey, old boy, where ya been?" I heard Billy say as he rubbed the dog's head. Well, where did Billy think he had been? I put my hands on my hips and stared. It was plain the dog adored Billy. "Go on, dog," Billy said, and pointed across at me. "Go for your walk." Old Wolf refused. Billy took him by the collar and led him back. "There you go, boy." He gave me the leash, but Old Wolf wasn't going anywhere without Billy.

We ended up walking him together. Billy was barefoot, even though the sidewalks would soon be blistering. "Where're your shoes?" I asked him.

"Savin' 'em," he said. "They're too good to wear now."

I saw him after that, but nothing regular. That was fine with me. I had other things to think about.

This was the first summer I had been allowed to stay home all day by myself. I liked the freedom, being trusted with it.

I had lots to do—tidy up the house, work in the Burts' garden, brush and walk Old Wolf, write to Jeff, read in the mulberry tree, roller-skate and ride my bike. I wrote penny postcards to Mrs. Burt, telling her what flowers were blooming in her yard and what was turning ripe in the garden. She wrote to tell us how Mr. Burt was doing.

Some days Maria and I walked to town for a Popsicle or to read the funny books at Rexall if the druggist wasn't looking. Other days I helped her take care of her baby brothers, but I didn't stay long. Maria's house smelled like wet diapers and spit-up milk.

Evenings I had some time in our own garden with Dad when he got home from work. We agreed, though: Hands off each other's tomatoes! A duel's a duel, we said. When we walked over to inspect the Burts' garden, I could tell Dad was amazed. "But those tomatoes," he'd say, shaking his head. "Pity."

"Pity you're going to lose!" I'd answer, and we'd walk back home, his big hand cradling the back of my neck.

The workroom off our kitchen became the Young Sprouts' headquarters. Thick leaves of mulberry outside the window and a row of elms shading the roof made this the coolest room in summer. Mother kept an old coffee can on the shelf. Miraculously, it sprouted new cookies each time we picked it clean.

When school had been out for several weeks I began to wonder where Billy was. Not that I cared, but Old Wolf would whine and paw the ground, looking for him, whenever we went out.

Then, early one morning when I was in the garden, up popped Billy and scared the living daylights out of me. "What the Sam Hill are you doin'?" he said. That must have been his pop's kind of talk.

I hadn't seen him coming. I was using the secret weapon. New blossoms were coming on all the time, and I had to do this when no one was around, since it was my secret, and Dad's. I thought better of saying it was none of his beeswax.

"Nothing," I said, but he had already seen.

"You gotta do this whole row? Clear to the alley?"

"Yes."

"Here." To my amazement, he held out his hand. "I'll do some."

He worked and I watched, and I told him I would wring his neck if he told anyone. " 'Twouldn't matter," he said. "This ain't gonna help."

"How do you know?"

"Just know. My grandma had tomatoes. She didn't do this. Hers were huge."

"Then why are you helping?"

"Just am."

I was determined not to argue with Billy. There'd be no winning. I had an idea. "If you like to work in the garden—" I began.

"Didn't say I liked it."

He left as abruptly as he had come.

"Thank you," I called to his back.

He turned his head, hunched a shoulder, and walked on.

I was sure the secret was safe with Billy. He seldom talked to anyone.

CHAPTER 15

Jeff's bicycle gave me a brand-new freedom, better than the roller skates I no longer missed. By July the sun beat down on Shady Grove as if to bake it brown, the gentle rains forgotten. When the house was sweltering, I left it and wheeled around town, loving the wind blowing through my hair. Even a hot breeze feels cool when you're sweating. One day, not in the mood for anything else, I rode everywhere—up around the courthouse, over to school and back, down past the corner lot.

I slowed at the depot. It looked different, smaller, than when we'd said goodbye to Jeff there. The junkyard lay beyond the depot. It was more than a junkyard, but not much more. At the front corner was a barn-red shanty. Jenkins Antiques was hand-painted on a board nailed to the door.

Everyone called the junkyard operator Junker, although I supposed he had some other first name. I had heard he went through the impossibly worn-out stuff people threw away and managed to rescue some of it. Anything that could be made to work, he set up on shelves and called antiques. I rode past quickly; it gave me the creeps.

Just past the junkyard the grain elevator towered against a blue sky. Beyond that lay a field of wheat, golden brown as Old Wolf's coat and tall as a baseball bat. The grain rippled in the wind. Oceans rippled like that, I'd heard. If Billy Riggs lived further out than this, he surely had a long walk to school. Without admitting to myself that I'd been looking for him, I turned around and pedaled back toward home.

Then I saw it, set back from the road, between the junkyard and the grain elevator. I'd missed it as I was going out. The house was more like a shack, the color of dirt, with shingles on the sides as well as on the roof. You couldn't tell where the junkyard ended and the shack's yard began. I thought I saw a curtain flapping through an open, screenless window. A rusty pump stood near the house. There really was a well. I shivered, remembering what Billy had said about his pop. I stomped on the pedals, sending spurts of gravel out from under my tires, and pumped with all my might.

Scott showed up at the garden on Saturday with a shiner as purple as plums.

"You, Walker? A black eye?" Andy sounded jealous.

Scott picked up a hoe and began hacking. I shot Andy a look, but he and the others were bound to stare at Scott until he explained.

"Had a run-in with Billy," he said.

"Riggs?" Andy's eyes were wide. He made a fist.

Scott shook his head. "My fault. I swung first."

"Wow!" said Andy. "Does he look as bad?"

"I wouldn't doubt it."

We saw that Scott didn't intend to explain further, but he saw that we didn't intend to let it go.

"Billy insulted my dad." He put a hand to his swollen eye. "Sometimes it *is* worth it," he said.

I wondered if Billy would ever show his face again after that, but I saw him one day from the mulberry tree. I was dying to ask him what he'd said—not that bluntly, of course. But I wasn't about to let him see my hiding place. I waited for him to pass by, then climbed down and went through the house to the front porch. He had to come back this way eventually.

I sat on the shady side and leafed through one of the *Life* magazines that had piled up in the living room. It was hard to get around to them all, since they came every week.

I caught my breath at a picture and its caption: *Germany's great naval base at Kiel is bombed by U.S. Liberators.* Great fists of smoke reached up from ships in a harbor, as though to clutch the airplanes overhead. I'd know those planes anywhere.

I felt numb. Which was I, really, proud or scared?

None of the stories in my scrapbook had pictures quite like this, and in the poster on my bedroom wall the B-24s were clean, in crisp colors, flying into a clear blue sky.

It didn't take long for Billy to come sauntering back by. He sported a wicked yellow circle around one eye. We talked about airplanes again. It seemed to be the only thing, other than tomatoes, that we could talk about. I should have known that would lead to a fight, but he didn't have to say what he said.

I was going on nervously about Jeff and his B-24 when Billy said, "Them bombers ain't so hot. They'd be dead without the Lightnings."

"They'd be what? How dare you?" I shouted.

I'll say this for Billy: He looked embarrassed when he realized what he'd said. And he didn't walk away.

"Well, not dead, but—well, yeah, probably."

"You're making that up!" I felt my face going red.

"Ain't neither. You ask your brother."

"I'm asking you. What's a Lightbeam, anyway?" I hated it that Billy knew something about planes that I didn't.

"Lightning. It's a Lockheed P-thirty-eight. Dandy little fighter plane, one of ours. Flies along to keep the Japanese Zero from shooting down your brother's B-twenty-four."

I hated him, but he wouldn't stop. "Not only that, some P-thirty-eights carry bombs of their own. That's the truth. I ain't makin' that up."

"How do you know this?"

"Just do. You ain't the only one knows stuff." Then he muttered, as if to himself, "You and that prissy Walker."

104

Aha. I was about to find out.

"Scott, prissy? Scott's the man of his house. He's responsible for his mom and three other kids. His dad is—"

"I know about his dad. Big deal."

I wanted to tell him that it *was* a big deal, that Scott's dad was making a sacrifice, and that Scott was, too. I wanted to say that he should be grateful his own dad was home. But he wouldn't have heard me. He didn't seem to like anyone, not Mr. Burt, not any of the kids, not Miss Elliott, whom everybody else liked, not my mother, who gave him chicken, nor my dad, who fixed his shoes.

"Look, I've tried to be nice to you," I said.

"Yeah. Tried. Like it was some stinking chore."

"Chore?" I glared.

"Yeah. Chore. You guys think you're better than anybody. You, always braggin' about your hero brother. Walker, lordin' it over everybody cuz his dad's in the army—"

I bit my tongue, hard. At least Scott's father wasn't a drunk. "Is that why you punched him?"

"He punched me."

"Okay. Is that why he punched you, 'cause his dad's in the army? 'Cause you don't like that? What's it to you, anyway?" I was shouting again.

Billy shot back, "Well, what's it to *you*?"

This time I did the leaving. I stomped into the house and banged the door shut. When I was sure Billy was gone, I went out back to the mulberry tree. I closed my eyes and tried to see Jeff soaring over Europe, free and high above the battle. The image would no longer come.

I went to his room. I could talk to him better there.

The plane on his wall mocked me. It was a box, just like Billy had said at the Bootery, chunkier than the sleeker, smaller models on Jeff's bookshelves and windowsills. Why did Jeff like it so much?

I knelt before the bookshelf and ran my finger along the books on the bottom shelf, tall books like the *Book of Knowledge* and Jeff's old notebooks. I pulled out some of the notebooks. They were filled with drawings of airplanes, hand-drawn maps with dotted lines marking famous flights and notes in Jeff's peculiar scrawl. He had pages and pages of the stuff. I'd never get through it to learn why this B-24 was so important.

A sheaf of notebook paper, folded lengthwise, fell out. A school assignment. On the half-sheet cover was printed:

AMERICAN AVIATION
AND
WHAT IT MEANS TO ME
Senior Paper
by
Jeffrey Alan Marks
May 15, 1941

That was just weeks before he went away. The teacher's handwriting under the date said, *A+ Good writing. Good luck up there.*

I unfolded it. *Aviation was born in 1903,* Jeff had written. *Only one other thing as important as that took place that year. My father was born.*

I hadn't thought of that. I read quickly through the first part. I had heard it many times: the Wright brothers' Flyer I with its motorcycle engine, flying from Kitty Hawk for almost one minute, reaching a height of fifteen feet.

More names I'd heard from Jeff and Dad: Eddie Rickenbacker, the Great War ace, resented by army brass who didn't have much use for airplanes and hated it that Rickenbacker got twice the pay of an army platoon leader. Billy Mitchell, outspoken in his call for more U.S. planes.

Then came several pages about transatlantic flights. I learned something new. Charles Lindbergh had not been the first to fly across the Atlantic, but he had been the first to fly alone, nonstop, and in a small airplane.

I sat on the floor, my back against the bookshelf, reading. *Twenty-four years after the Wrights' one-minute trip in their "flying motorcycle," Charles Lindbergh flew for thirty-three and a half hours, covering three thousand, six hundred miles. At that time, Jeffrey Alan Marks, future pilot, was four years old.*

Well! He was sure of himself, wasn't he? That was Jeff!

Less than a decade after Lindbergh's long flight across the sea, Amelia Earhart (from Kansas, incidentally) attempted a round-the-world flight and was lost. It was tragic, but Miss Earhart flew for the best reason anyone has ever had: She loved it.

I decided not to ponder Amelia's fate. Finally I found what I was looking for.

In January 1939, General Henry H. "Hap" Arnold

asked the Consolidated Aircraft Company to design a bomber
superior to the B-17. It had to go faster, further and higher.
It was the B-24.

So there, Billy Riggs!

It did all those things, but was not quite as steady.

Oh, well.

*The bomb bay has room for eight thousand pounds of ex-
plosives.*

Well, that would take a box!

*Consolidated Aircraft built the first B-24s, in San Diego,
California, and sold them to Great Britain, already at war
with Germany. The British flew the first B-24 just four
months before I sat down to write this paper. They call it the
Liberator. It is the biggest, best bomber yet, and I am going to
fly one someday.*

I didn't find anything about P-38s in Jeff's report.
Did Billy know what he was talking about? I decided to
ask Jeff, and pulled out a blank V-mail sheet.

Dear Jeff,

*Thanks for your letter. I've saved all your let-
ters in the cedar box you gave me one Christmas.*

*The gardens are growing. We tried to make
Mother say which side she was on, but she ducked.
She's neutral, she says.*

*The kids are making money! Every week we
pay the* Chronicle *for our ad and go to the Guaranty Bank to buy our stamps. We keep a nickel
apiece out for ice cream, and hit the Sweet Shoppe.*

Then I told him what Billy had said, and about how Billy was so hard to understand sometimes. *Why do some people just want to make trouble, Jeff?* I wrote. I had rambled on to the bottom of the page, so I ended with, *I'll explain the secret weapon in my next letter.*

I'd cooled off some by the time I'd finished the letter and gone out to my bike. Billy was always walking off, but he'd never stomped away screaming mad, except when Andy had bloodied his shirt. Maybe I was the one who started our arguments. Maybe I owed him an apology.

I kicked up the stand, jumped on a pedal, and threw my leg over the bar. The bike lurched and wobbled under me. I turned around to look at the back tire. Flat. The bicycle pump didn't help. The tire would not hold the air. I knew there were no new bicycle tires to be had in Shady Grove. If you couldn't get one you just had to abandon your bike for the duration. I wondered how I had ever lived without mine, and how I ever could again.

I thought of walking Old Wolf out past Billy's, finding a way to make conversation. But I remembered what Billy had said. His pop would kick a dog down the well. Besides, it was scorching hot outside. Maybe I'd wait for a cooler day.

The next day was no cooler. I sat on the front porch reading the *Chronicle*, Old Wolf stretched out at my feet. I always read the local news first. Who had out-of-town company? Who had a new baby? What were the ladies' clubs doing? Sometimes Mother's name was there, along with those of other wives: *Mrs. Alan Marks, Mrs. Ben Knorr and Mrs. James Bowen attended a Red Cross class.* I wondered why the women were called by their husbands' names instead of their own. My own name had been there, in the Young Sprouts story.

The new paperboy never stopped to talk, and I sorely missed Kuppa. So when Billy shuffled up the walk, I was just glad to see somebody.

"Hi," I said, wondering what had brought him around again.

"Hi." He had one arm behind him. "Brought you something." He turned around so I could see it.

I couldn't think of anything to say as I reached for the thin balsa model, a twin-tailed B-24.

"It's from a cereal box, but it's wood, and I put it together myself," he said. "Thought you'd like it."

"I do. Thanks." I blinked hard.

Billy rubbed Old Wolf's head. "Okay if I run him?"

"Sure."

"You could ride along on your bike," he said, giving me a sideways glance.

"I can't. It has a flat."

"Let's see."

I wheeled the bike around from the back. Billy tried the tire pump, but I was right. Air leaked out again.

"Where's that tub we washed Old Wolf in?"

By the time I had brought the tub around and filled it from the hose, Billy had the tire off the wheel and the tube pulled out of it. He pressed the tube into the water, moving it so that only a part of it was under at one time. Finally tiny bubbles floated up to the surface.

"There's your problem, a hole. Got any chalk?"

I found some in Mother's sewing box. He took the tube out and dried off the offending spot with his shirttail. "Hold on to it right here," he said. He marked the spot with the chalk, then pulled something out of his pocket. "This'll do it."

Now, how did he just happen to have a tire patch in his overall pocket? And glue?

"Let 'er get good and dry," he said when he finished. He set the tube aside and ran his hands around the tire. "Thought so. You picked up an old shingle nail." He pulled it out with his teeth. "These are devils," he said between his teeth, then spat the nail into his hand. "Happens all the time." He bounced the nail in his hand. "Got a lot of these out by the junkyard."

I ducked my head. "Thanks for fixing it," I said. "For the plane, too."

"Sure." He whistled for Old Wolf. "Come on, dog. Let's run."

As I watched them tear off, I counted the good things Billy had done for me: found Old Wolf, walked him, helped with the secret weapon, brought me a present and fixed my tire. In between times he just dropped out of sight. What would he be up to next?

I carried the airplane inside as carefully as if it had been a baby bird and put it on Jeff's dresser. That seemed to be where it belonged.

CHAPTER 16

It was mid-July, hot and dry. We might have had second thoughts, but we worked until we wilted—it was us or the garden. How we longed for rain! The first welcome drops fell on hot sidewalks, the walks people said you could fry an egg on. Then, like a pushy guest, the rain stayed on and took over.

Lying in bed one night, I watched the storm. Lightning tore the black sky. Thunder rumbled in and roared out. It sounded like war. I fell asleep imagining Jeff and Scott's father and the gardens all being bombed with rain.

The next morning I lifted a raincoat from a hook in the workroom and pulled on galoshes. Outside, I bent into the slashing rain and crossed the street. Wind lashed the branches of the Burts' giant elm. Just weeks before, the Sprouts had sat under that tree and planned how we would market our crops. Now the crops were awash in more water than the ground could hold.

Perhaps the garden would survive, except for the lettuce, but there would be no picking or weeding soon. We'd have an enforced vacation.

Glad of a lazy morning, I tidied the living room and sprawled on the sofa with a pile of magazines. I thumbed through one looking at pictures. One full page featured Fala, the president's little black Scottie. Another showed Bob Hope advertising Pepsodent. Then a headline leaped out: "Floods Ravage Midwest Farms." We were not the only soggy ones. *Millions of acres under water . . . peril to the nation's food supply . . . Department of Agriculture getting supplies to farmers for reseeding.* I could just see Andy demanding that they replace our lettuce.

The streets dried before the gardens did, at least enough for bike riding. I rode through the puddles, remembering Jeff and grateful for Billy. The tire, its tube patched and sealed, held up fine.

I hadn't accounted for old age—the bike's age. The chain snapped when I jumped a curb. It would take a new chain or bicycle repair shop, Dad said later. That would mean a trip into the city, an impossibility except for emergencies. As if this weren't one!

When, after two weeks away, the Sprouts got back into the garden, I was suddenly too busy to worry about a bike. We groaned when we saw what lay before us! Until then we had merely picked. That day we would harvest!

Beets, carrots, peas, beans, peppers, cucumbers and turnips piled up on the workroom counter. We filled arm baskets and paper sacks and set out in teams. Maria, Ellie and I pulled the *Flying Thunder*, Jeff's old wagon, loaded down. The boys struck out on bikes, baskets jammed full.

By now, the outdoors felt like a steam kettle ready for new corn, but we pushed on, determined to sell everything. It took until seven at night, and when we gathered at the garden again the next day, it seemed as if we had just been there. Scott whistled. "And we thought yesterday was a long day! Were these all here then?"

Weeds towered through the plants and sprouted between the rows. Breezeless air, hot and muggy, made it our most miserable Saturday. Mud oozed between our bare toes while we slapped at mosquitoes and decided where to begin.

A weed slipped out of my hands when I pulled at it. I didn't want to be the prodder that day, the one to keep the gang going. "We'll never get them all," I moaned.

"Sure we will," said Maria. "The ground is soft." She gripped a weed and pulled straight up. "See? Where's the weed basket?"

"Here!" said Ellie. She headed for Maria with the bushel basket. Suddenly she dropped it, screamed and ran.

Andy scrambled for the basket and turned it over and over. "Nothing here. She probably saw a bug."

I read Maria's thought in her look. Honestly! I left my trowel by a half-dug weed and stood up, intending to follow Ellie. In midstep I stopped, gasped and caught myself at the elbows. Head still, neck stiff, I lowered my eyes.

No one else moved. Then a sudden, slithering streak set them all in motion. Andy reached for a hoe, but Scott clutched his shoulder.

"Let it go," he said. "It's just a garter snake, harmless. They get into gardens sometimes."

"Don't tell Ellie that," said Andy. "Tell her it's a Gobi Desert snake and there'll never be one here again."

"Better tell her the truth." Scott spoke quietly. "I'll do it. My mom's afraid of snakes, too." He began a slow walk toward Ellie. My grateful look followed him. I unwound my arms, but my knees were shaking.

The others tore into the weeds as if their lives depended on getting done and getting out. They talked like nervous first graders on opening day, and even Andy sneaked looks from side to side as he worked. Only Scott and Ellie, who had come back with him, seemed calm. Whatever he'd said to her, he should have said to all of us.

Billy came shuffling by just as I was crossing the street with the hoe.

"You should have come earlier. You missed the excitement." I told him about the snake.

He grinned. "Yeah, I would've liked that."

"We could've used some help, too. We had a jungle of weeds."

"Oh, no. You ain't roping me into that."

"I just thought—"

"I know you believe in that stuff, bein' patriotic, bringin' the men back and all. It probably will."

"Then why...," I began, but stopped. Billy had

shoved his hands into his pockets and pressed his lips together, like he was trying not to say more. "You can tell me," I said.

His words came out like a breath held too long. "Ain't no garden in the world gonna bring my pop back."

"Your pop's gone?"

"Been gone a long time, in a way. Somewheres only he knows where. Somewheres in his own head. 'Cept sometimes he's here, like when we fish or when he's telling me about the last war. But mostly he's gone. No garden's gonna change that."

We decided to take telephone orders to speed things up. I agreed we could use my number, and Andy's dad paid to have "Call 55" added to our *Chronicle* ad.

The next time we picked, I lined empty sacks up on the workroom counter and labeled each sack with a customer's name and order: D. MARTIN, 2 CUCUMBERS, 4 CARROTS, 1 ONION. When we got back to the workroom after picking, we walked past the sacks like we were playing musical chairs and filled them directly from our baskets.

When we had delivered the order sacks and peddled the remaining vegetables door to door, we still had time for a game of work-up. We fed the quart jar, shook it, and cheered. We had survived drought, rain, sun, mosquitoes, bugs, one snake and Theda Buell. Who said we couldn't do it?

A week later Scott came down with the mumps. His

mom called just as we were heading over to the garden. "Scott says he has orders for new potatoes," she said. "We're really sorry."

"Mumps, now?" said Andy as we trudged across the street, tools in tow. "Poor guy. I had mumps in first grade." So had the rest of us.

Scott's potatoes could be left in the ground for weeks, I knew. But he had promised the customers those tiny new ones, dug while still a pinkish red.

I was beginning to feel like Tom Sawyer in reverse, doing more, not less. With Mrs. Burt's flowers, the tomatoes, the telephone orders and extra work when one of the Young Sprouts missed a day, I barely had time to do my house chores and write to Jeff. I spent little time in our own garden now, leaving most of it up to Dad.

Still, I was better off than Scott. I left a wide space between the potato fork and the plant as I dug, so I wouldn't slice into the potatoes, and knelt to pull out the smallest ones. I counted out six to take to Scott. He should have them, even if he couldn't eat them.

Covered with dirt but too tired to wash, I delivered them to Scott's back door. His mother answered, her face drawn, her shoulders slumped. I thought she would be a pretty woman ordinarily. Scott's little sister, in dirty rompers, clung to her. Two small boys tugged at her dress. I must have stared. Two little faces, round as pumpkins, jaws swollen up to their temples.

Mrs. Walker smiled a weak smile. "Yes," she said. "Three mumps faces in one house. You boys get back in bed, now. You have to stay down." To me she said in the same breath, "I hope you've had mumps."

"I have. I brought Scott the first potatoes out of the garden. And please tell him we have enough to fill his orders. I'll deliver them after supper."

"Bless you! He'll be so pleased, but I'm sure he won't let you see him." She pointed to her cheeks. "I'll see if he has a message."

While I waited on the porch, I looked at the garden that ran along the back of the house. It was obvious no one had worked on it since the rains. Weeds had shot up everywhere. A black garden hose, unneeded for weeks, lay neglected among the plants.

Scott's words came back to me. "My mom says it's the decent thing to do," he had said when I asked for volunteers, a hundred years ago, it seemed. Their garden would soon be overgrown. Someone had to do the decent thing for them now.

Mrs. Walker returned with a note. In scraggly letters, it said:

> *Thanks Treese*
> *Your all right*
> *Scott*

"The Walkers' garden is small," I said to Mother later in the kitchen. "We could do it in half the time we do the Burts' if everyone helped." I snapped the ends off the string beans from that day's picking. "But I've pushed the Sprouts pretty hard."

"Hmm." Mother held up her cooking spoon. "Maybe you can pull them this time."

"Pull them?"

It came up again at supper. "You mean offer them something they can't resist? I don't have money to pay them. I'm sure Mrs. Walker doesn't, either."

"And Charley Sweet has already donated ice cream cones once," Mother said. She smiled as she passed the beans to Dad.

Dad stopped his fork between his plate and his mouth.

"Ice cream! We haven't had that ice cream freezer out in ages!"

I was on the phone before the table was cleared.

The promise of homemade ice cream canceled any other plans. Every Sprout except Scott crowded onto our small back porch with my mother and dad on Sunday afternoon. They took turns turning the handle of the freezer and feeding it ice and salt. When the handle would barely move, Dad pronounced the ice cream done. "Hot diggety," said Andy.

Mother removed the lid and the paddle. She scraped the paddle, leaving some of the sweet stuff on it for tastes. Replacing the lid, she said, "It has to sit in the tub for an hour or so. What would you like to do while you wait?" She glanced at me.

"Let's go see Scott," I said. "We can take flowers from Mrs. Burt's yard."

"Boys don't like flowers," said Andy.

"Boys' mothers do," said Mother.

Since the flowers were for Scott's mother, the boys helped pick them. Then Ellie, Andy, Maria and I cut through the alley and trooped over to Scott's.

Andy stuck his hand out with the flowers and made the presentation speech to Mrs. Walker. "For you. From us."

"Oh, you kids. Thank you! I'm afraid Scott's asleep. I'll tell him you stopped by." As she closed the screen door, I saw a smile on her face that hadn't been there before. She really was pretty.

The Walkers' garden filled their small backyard from door to alley. As we filed down the back path, I leaned over a tomato plant to pull a weed. "Look at all these!" I said. I caught Andy's glance and circled the air with my finger, nodding toward the other kids.

"Hey, this is right up our alley," said Andy. He bent over the next row. "Well, Scott's alley." Andy wouldn't miss a chance to clown. It always worked. "Tell you what. Everybody take a row. First one done gets double ice cream," he called.

I hoped the ice cream would hold out.

It did. There was even enough to take some back over to Scott after Andy got the double portion, proving himself a better weed puller than he had ever let us know.

* * *

Billy had disappeared again. A letter came back from Jeff with the answers to my questions.

> *Your friend is right, Teresa. Those Lightnings have saved my skin a time or two. We're lucky to have them. Don't worry about me, squirt. I've got a good bird, and Billy's P-38s are there.*
>
> *About your friend, when people act like they want trouble, it's often because they've already got trouble. Billy's a fighter, sounds like. Nothing wrong with that if you know what's worth fighting for.*
>
> *Love,*
> *Jeff*

CHAPTER 17

I checked the Burts' tomatoes every morning. When the ground dried again, I gave them a thorough soaking. Orange deepened into red, and at last there were ripe tomatoes to sell. To my surprise, Theda Buell was the first to phone for them. But the very first one was for me! I pulled it off the vine, rubbed the dirt off on my overalls, and bit in, letting juice run down my chin.

We hadn't gone to Miss Buell's house, at the other end of town, since the green pepper episode. I chose three tomatoes for her, the biggest and reddest ones after the one I'd eaten. If I delivered them that day, we could save time on our regular pick-and-sell day. Tomatoes were best if picked the day they became ripe. Surely even the most disagreeable customer would appreciate that.

But Miss Buell didn't! "You're early," she said when she opened her door.

I had hiked all the way across town, but I checked my tongue. Then I had an inspiration: I would imagine I was talking to Mrs. Burt!

"These are our first tomatoes. I brought them as soon as they were ready," I said, pretending to enjoy myself.

"Ad said Friday. Come back tomorrow."

There was only one Mrs. Burt. On the other hand, there was only one Miss Buell.

I got up early on Friday and walked, again, the twelve blocks to her house.

"Will you be wanting something next week?" I asked her after she paid me.

"Tomatoes again."

"Thank you. I'll see that you get them. Usually Scott Walker delivers in this area, but he's sick today."

"Walker? That kid whose dad signed up?"

"For the army? Yes, ma'am. Scott—"

"Humph." The woman sniffed. "Man ought to be taking care of his family."

"He *is* taking care of his family," I said, suddenly emboldened. "He's keeping our country safe for them."

Her mouth fell open, but she said nothing.

"I'll bring the tomatoes myself," I said.

$\mathcal{I}$ had told Jeff enough of my troubles in my last letter, so I wouldn't bother him with Miss Buell. But I had to tell him about eating that first tomato right there in the

Burts' garden and how sweet it tasted. *And I didn't even have to steal it,* I teased. Then I answered the question he had asked. I had to write small.

> *I said I'd explain the secret weapon. Well, long story. One day after you left I was picking flowers with Mrs. Burt. I was afraid of the bees (remember, I was smaller then), but she just moved quietly while we talked about the colors and sniffed the blossoms. She said we needed bees to spread the pollen and make the flowers grow.*
>
> *Later, I noticed there were no bees in our garden. How could the pollen spread from one yellow tomato blossom to another? I wondered.*
>
> *I went indoors to paint in my coloring book. I was dabbing color here and there, painting flowers. The picture had a bumblebee in one corner. And that made me think! I could take a paintbrush from an old watercolor set and dab it from one tomato blossom to another, and another. That would spread the pollen, just like the bees spread it among Mrs. Burt's flowers.*
>
> *Dad liked it! He said, "That's very clever. We'll make it our secret weapon." We tried it, and our tomatoes beat Mr. Burt's—twice! I miss you.*
>
> *Love,*
> *Teresa*

I detested searching for hornworms—running my hands around in the thick vines, checking for black holes bored in the tomatoes. Some days Billy came by and helped me. He had reappeared. We imprisoned the worms in a can with a lid. Later, I'd throw them into the fire when Dad burned the trash in the metal barrel behind our house.

Even with all that care, I found two of the Burts' tomatoes one day with ugly splits in their skins. This was not from hornworms. I had done everything right: kept the weeds down and the pests out, given plenty of water when the rain dried up. What had happened?

I sat down, cross-legged, deflated, and shook my fist at the plants. "You!" I sputtered. I couldn't tell Dad about this.

I pulled the split tomatoes off and struck out kittycorner across town. My feet were my only means of transportation now, and the greenhouse was clear over by Theda Buell's, as far as it could be and still be in town. But Mr. Tiller was my only hope.

My legs were burning inside my overalls when I stepped into the small office space at the front. The musty smell of damp soil came through the doorway from the back.

"Look!" I said when Mr. Tiller stepped through. I lifted a shoulder, wiped the sweat off my face with my sleeve and held out the tomatoes.

"Read about you in the paper, Teresa," he said, taking the tomatoes. "That's a good thing you kids are doing."

"Thank you," I said, but I didn't want to talk about the Young Sprouts just then.

He turned the tomatoes over in his palms and

studied them. "Mm-hmm," he said, like a doctor looking down a sore throat.

"Are they all going to split?"

"Depends." He set the tomatoes on a cluttered desk. "We had lots of rain a while back, remember?"

"Yes."

"And then a long hot spell."

"Right."

"Did you water really, really well after it got hot?"

"I did, I swear I did!"

"That's what I thought. Let me show you something." He led me through the doorway and down a dirt aisle. Plants of all kinds sat in pots on either side. Sunlight filtered through a glass ceiling that had been brushed with white paint. We stopped at the tomatoes. Mr. Tiller pointed. "See this?"

The tomato was perfect, almost ripe, with only a thin ring of green around the stem. My split tomatoes had looked like that a few days earlier.

"The thing that makes the tomato swell up to its full size is . . ."

"Water," I said.

"Right. Like air going into a balloon, water goes into the tomato, stretching its skin. What happens when you get too much air in the balloon? Pop!"

"Too much water? Then they'll all go bad!"

"I don't think so. Tell you what," he said. "Take a shovel. Dig down a little way into the ground beside the plant with the split tomatoes. Then dig beside one of the others."

"Okay, but—"

"If the soil is wetter, and wet further into the ground, beside the plant that had the split tomatoes, chances are that plant got more water than the others. It happens."

"So the others might be okay?"

"I'm betting on it." He reached across the dirt aisle and snapped a long stem of purple larkspur. "My favorite flower. For you, for your hard work. You've been busy as the bees that bring the flowers."

I laughed. "And the tomatoes?"

His answer made me reel.

"No, not the tomatoes. Tomatoes don't need bees."

"Why not?"

"Tomatoes are self-pollinated. The pollen in the blossom just drops down further inside. That starts the tomato."

"Oh," I said.

"Something wrong?" He was looking at me, his head bent to one side like a drooping hollyhock.

"Oh, no. Thank you for the help, and for the larkspur."

I stumbled out. My eyes were hot in my head. I ran, not to get anywhere but just to get away. Away from myself and my stupid ideas. I slowed down in the last block and dropped, panting, under the Burts' shade tree.

At least we had kept it a secret, if Riggs hadn't blabbed. Billy was right; it didn't help. But if it wasn't the secret weapon, what had made the difference between our tomatoes and Burt's?

I gasped for breath. Heavens! It was dumb luck.

I fumed! How could my own father have let me believe it was the paintbrushes and go on "pollinating" through two more summers? I must be as dumb as he thought I was, to fall for that. What would I tell Jeff?

A voice interrupted my thoughts. "Excuse me. Teresa?"

I swung around. "Oh, Kenneth, you scared me. Did we order something?"

Kenneth was the teenager who delivered small orders for the IGA. He straddled his bike.

"No. I'm looking for Mrs. Scott Walker. Can you tell me where she lives? I've never delivered anything to her." His voice cracked, and his face looked white as chalk dust. There were no groceries in his bicycle basket. Panic gripped me as it all came together.

Few telegrams came to Shady Grove. When one did, the Teletype operator rang for Kenneth at the IGA. While everyone loved Kenneth, no one wanted to see him at the front door without groceries.

"I'll show you," I said when I found my voice. I walked ahead of him and pointed. "Two blocks. Yellow house. On the corner."

As he pedaled off, I couldn't stop myself. "What does it say?" I shouted.

Over his shoulder he called, "I'm not allowed to read 'em."

I watched the bicycle. It swam away through a deep pool, pulling me under with it. When I came up, struggling for air, I realized I'd only been holding my breath. But everything had changed.

I stumbled across the street and scaled the mulberry tree. I was an idiot. I'd believed in secret weapons. I'd believed that paintbrushes pollinate tomatoes. I'd believed in gardens and war stamps and doing the decent thing. I'd even believed that tomatoes held sway over life and death.

I let the truth slam into my chest, the awful truth I had buried inside. Men were not spared because they were fathers. Brothers were not safe because they were in the air. It wasn't just Sonny Ferguson. The war wasn't finished with us yet. I put my head in my arms and sobbed.

CHAPTER 18

"Diggin' tomatoes?" Billy's voice startled me. "Aren't you confused?" he said, scratching his grubby head.

"Just stupid. I overwatered, and the tomatoes from this plant split open." I explained Mr. Tiller's theory. Billy squatted and poked his fingers into the soil. "This is still damp. Is it supposed to be?"

"It should be dry by now. I have to find out if all the plants got as soaked as this one."

"Here," he said, reaching for the spade. It still surprised me when he offered to help. He walked a few paces and dug in another spot. "Stuff's dry here. I'd say you're safe."

"Wow. Thanks," I said. If he had been a girl, I'd have hugged him.

He shrugged, but he didn't turn away. He made no move to leave, just put his hands in his pockets and stood there. "You don't look happy. Thinking about Scott's dad?" he asked me. Billy didn't look so grimy when you looked right into his eyes, when he let you.

"Yes." I wondered how Billy had heard. It wasn't quite as bad as I had imagined. Mr. Walker wasn't dead, but he was missing in action.

"We can fix your watering problem," Billy said.

"We can?"

"I'll be back in a jiffy. Wait here."

"Well, now, where would I be goin'?" I said, and we both smiled, remembering the day he had found Old Wolf.

Billy never did anything in a jiffy except maybe throw his fists, but he might come back.

Andy, Maria and Ellie showed up, looking glum. They too had heard about Scott's father. "He'll probably stay with his mom today," said Andy. "If it was my mom, she wouldn't let me out of her sight."

I drew their attention away. I told them about the split tomatoes and what Mr. Tiller had said about uneven watering. The tomatoes were theirs, too, so I had to tell them. I didn't have to mention the so-called secret weapon. It hadn't made any difference, anyway.

I didn't mention Billy, either. He might not even come back.

He did, though, dragging an old garden hose, a short board and a hammer. He stopped when he saw the other kids. He looked at his stuff, must have decided it was too much to drag back, and kept coming.

"Billy's going to help us," I said.

"What's he got?" said Andy.

"I'm not sure."

The kids hung back. Billy didn't say much. He just went to work. He stretched a section of hose over the board.

"Where'd you get this?" I asked him.

"Just got it. Hold it tight," he said. He punched holes in the hose, tapping a very thin nail with the hammer.

"The holes have to be tiny, and lots of them," he said. "It's called a soaker hose."

By now, the others were leaning over us, curious.

"Are you sure the water will come through?" I asked.

"I'm sure, and it seeps right down to the roots." He looked up, over our shoulders, and cocked his head. Someone was coming.

Scott pedaled up, braked his bike slowly and straddled it, leaning on the handlebars. The Sprouts shifted uneasily, glancing from Scott to Billy. I wondered if Billy would turn and walk away. Billy was made of better stuff than that. He held a hand out to Scott. "Bad deal about your dad," he said, which was as close as he could come to saying he was sorry.

"Thanks." Scott shook hands, looking off to the side.

I couldn't say it, either. I hoped Scott would see it in my face.

Not knowing what else to say, I said, "Look what Billy did." The soaker hose gave us all something to talk about, Billy, Scott, me and the other Sprouts. I was thinking how that had never happened. Pretty soon we were all explaining Mr. Tiller's theory to Scott, and Billy was explaining how the soaker hose worked.

"How did you know about this?" I asked him.

For once he told me. "Learned it from my grandma. The best part is, you don't have to stand and hold the hose."

"I wonder why Mr. Burt never told us about this."

"Huh. Why does he do anything? All's he has to do is his garden. I reckon he'd water it with a teaspoon if he had to." I laughed, picturing that. The others laughed with me, even Scott.

We strung the hose along a row of tomatoes and turned the water on to test it.

"Just remember, it all goes to the roots, so don't overdo it," said Billy.

"Thanks, Billy," I said.

"Good going, Riggs," said Andy.

"Nice work," said Scott.

"Sure," said Billy. He tapped Scott's arm with a loose fist. "Your dad's gonna be okay," he said. Then he ambled off.

Scott stayed after the others left. I guess he knew I would come closest to knowing how he really felt.

"Thanks for helping with our garden," he said.

"Sure. Everyone over the mumps?"

"So far. Cassie didn't get them."

"How's your mom?"

"I left her in the garden. She says it keeps her sane."

"Does she need a soaker hose? We know how to make one now."

"I don't think so. She likes to hold the hose. I watch her face sometimes when she's watering. She's kind of smiling, like when she reads Dad's letters. What she needs is a cure for weeds. She was about to give up before the Sprouts came over."

"Does she believe the victory gardens help the war effort?"

"With all her heart."

"I wish I did. After Jeff went away, I thought if we just had good enough tomatoes and string beans and stuff, he'd come back."

Scott smiled. "Well, not quite."

We talked about the gardens. I wondered out loud if it helped Mr. Burt to know his garden was being tended.

"It gives him something to think about, anyway," said Scott. "Sometimes you have to have something to think about." Scott was wiser than most boys. Most were just ornery.

"By the way, what did you say to Ellie about that snake?" I asked him.

"Oh, that. I told her what my dad told me before he went away. He said, 'The being scared is worse than what you're scared of. You and your mama remember that while I'm gone.' We're trying to now. Maybe he's already shown up somewhere." He toed his kickstand up, ready to go. He squeezed the handlebars, then pedaled away.

Who was worse off, Scott or Billy? I thought I knew. I looked at Billy's soaker hose again. An idea crept into my mind.

CHAPTER 19

$\mathcal{I}$ pulled the *Flying Thunder*, little clods of dirt falling over its sides, the spade rattling against the metal. Morning sounds played like music. Birds twittered, frogs croaked, a train whistled out in the distance. I walked with the early sun at my back, stepping carefully, watching for shingle nails. I knew what I was doing this time.

Billy's house looked better in the softer light of morning, until I got right up to it. I left the wagon off to the side and went around to the back door. I lifted my hand to knock, eager to tell Billy I'd brought him something. Maybe he would like it as much as I liked his airplane.

Only then did it occur to me that it might not be Billy who answered the door. Did he have a nice mother? She hadn't returned our platter. It wasn't that we minded the platter; it was just that mothers were usually so careful about things like that. Billy had never said one word about his mother, much as I had hinted. I sure didn't want to see his father. I let my hand fall.

The door stood open. The screen door hung by one hinge, making a gap, letting me see into the kitchen. There was no sound of people. I curved my hands around my eyes and leaned in for a better look. My first thought was that I didn't want the platter to come back from here. The kitchen looked like the junkyard. Dirty clothes and newspapers littered the floor. Dishes, chipped and unwashed, sat on the table with greasy machine parts and open cereal boxes. The sink had all but disappeared under dirty pots and empty cans. There was a pump over the sink where a faucet should have been.

"Lookin' fer somethin'?"

I whirled around, my elbow knocking the screen further askew.

"Yes," I said, my heart pounding. "I'm looking for you, Billy." It came out high and pleading.

"You ride out?"

"Walked. I brought you something. Over here."

I gestured toward the *Thunder.*

"You givin' me a wagon?"

"No." I hadn't thought he'd think that. I stammered, "I—I can't. It's Jeff's. I'm giving you what's in it." We were walking toward it.

"I was just teasin'. What is it?"

I don't know what I expected, that his eyes would go soft or he would whistle or maybe say "hot diggety" like

Andy always does. He said, "What the Sam Hill am I gonna do with that?"

"Plant it." I waited, but he just looked at the tomato plant in the wagon. I saw it through his eyes. Dry, smelly leaves, already wilting. Roots straggling out of the clump of dirt I had dug up with it. "It will make you feel closer to your grandma."

"Huh," he said, but it didn't have that hard bullet edge to it. "We ain't even got a hose here. Nothin' to hook it up to."

I hated the tears that were gathering in my eyes. "You got a well," I said.

"Hey, yeah, I do, don't I?" Something funny in his voice made me look up, even if he would see my tears. Clean white lines streaked down his dirty face.

We both laughed and ran for the well. Billy filled a battered pail, then lifted a tin cup from where it hung by a wire on the pump handle. He let the cup run over with cool water, then held it out to me. "Want a drink?" After my long walk and with the lump in my throat, there was nothing I wanted more. I swallowed the water in long noisy gulps, handed the cup back to Billy and wiped my mouth with the back of my hand.

We dug near a corner of the house, where the plant would get the afternoon sun. Two tomatoes clung to the vine, one green, one red. Merry Christmas, I almost said, wondering why I'd thought of that in the middle of summer, wondering if Billy ever got anything for Christmas.

He walked me back out to the road.

* * *

The thin, three-corner folded *Chronicle* hit the front porch with a soft thud. The boy didn't look up to say hello, just walked on, folding the next paper as he went. I picked it up, reading the Young Sprouts' ad on the triangle of back page and undoing the folds. I always read it back to front, three-line want ads and large store advertisements on the back page, then in the middle the local news, a picture or two, the garden column and more big ads. I read every word, not that there were many.

Closing it to read the front page last, I hesitated. This was strange. Heavy black lines outlined a square in the center of page one. I bent to read the words there. *With deepest regret, the editor and staff of the* Chronicle *must report news just in as we go to press. Laurence Coffey, son of Mr. and Mrs. J. L. Coffey, has been killed in action.*

Kuppa. There was more, but what was the use of reading it? I buried my face in the paper, clutching it in wads at my ears. When I couldn't breathe I threw the paper down and just started running, down the steps, past our garden, to the end of the block, to the softball lot and on. Words echoed in my head. *Need some help? Hey, Kuppa, yeah!* "Enlist and you get what you want," he'd told us. That's not what he wanted, my feet said as they pounded the road. This wasn't what Kuppa wanted.

I slowed to a walk as I neared the Riggses' place. Billy hadn't been around since we'd planted the tomato.

Did he hate it? Or was he just being here-again-gone-again Billy again? I doubted if he ever knew Laurence Coffey, but Billy was the only person I wanted to talk to. I turned in, picking my way through the weeds and trash up to his house.

I leaned over the withering tomato plant and cried. I knew I should leave, but I stamped around back, my face hot and wet. The screen door had come clear off and had fallen over the narrow steps leading up to it. I pushed it aside and pounded on the door. I tried the knob. I went around and tried the front door, twisting the knob, slapping the wood with one hand. The windows were closed, no curtain slipping out, flapping.

I should have noticed first thing that the pail and cup were gone from the well. The handle worked hard, but I managed to pump some water into a rusty bucket I found at the edge of the junkyard. I hurried with the bucket, one hand stretched out for balance, everything blurred around me. "It all goes to the roots, so don't overdo it," Billy had told me. I scooped the water out with my hands and dropped it around the plant, close in under the drooping leaves.

One tomato, ready to ripen, clung to a sagging branch. A few drying blossoms fluttered in the breeze.

"Don't die," I whispered.

I wrote to Jeff, but I didn't tell him any of the bad stuff. I told him Mr. Burt was almost well, that Dad would go to get him and Mrs. Burt when the time came. That we had saved our gas ration stamps for this. That the gardens were fine and the tomato duel was heating up. I finished with *Dad and I looked over both gardens together last night. We agreed our tomatoes are neck and neck. It will just depend on who happens to have the best ones come ripe on judging day!*

I began to think more about the duel than the war. "Sometimes you need something to think about," Scott had said. But the talk around town was still of the war, still punctuated with "get it over soon."

What "soon" meant, nobody knew, but things began to sound better. The latest news had captured everyone's attention: Operation Husky.

The headline shouted, "Allies Win Ten Cities; Yanks Hurl Back Fierce Attack." No landing force had ever been so large. Massive numbers of Allied ships, planes and troops had advanced across the Mediterranean Sea's largest island, Sicily, just off the toe of Italy. The place I was going to go someday.

When it was over, General Dwight D. Eisenhower said, "By golly, by golly, we've done it again!"

There was more. B-24s had struck the German-controlled oil facilities again at Ploesti. A triumphant headline announced, "Staggering Attack on Nazi Supply May Turn Course of War."

Did "soon" at last mean soon?

The walk to Billy's house seemed shorter now that I was used to it. Old Wolf pranced out ahead, barking at cars, raising puffs of dust with his paws. He was strong again, but he still whined for Billy when I took him out on the leash. We walked out every other day, and I checked the single tomato plant. The shack hunkered further down into the weeds. No cup at the well, no footprint in the dust, no flapping curtain at the window hinted of people.

I dribbled some water over the plant, wishing it had all turned out better. Billy wasn't the judge's son. Or Mr. Walker. Or even Kuppa. Billy was my friend, my age, my loss. In all of his disappearing days, I had never suspected that he wouldn't show up again eventually.

He was carrying on somewhere, I supposed. Scott was carrying on, too. So were his mom and my parents. "I guess it's time to grow up, Wolfie," I said. Who knew that could be so hard?

The day came for the Young Sprouts to make our final war stamp purchases. We met at the *Chronicle* and paid for the next ad. The rest of the money from the garden would be ours for rides and eats at the Harvest Festival. We went to Guaranty Bank and bought our stamps. The teller grinned as she counted them out. "You kids really did it!" she said. Carefully pocketing our stamps, we tore off to the Sweet Shoppe.

Charley Sweet leaned over our table. "You guys have been my best customers this summer," he said. We had—almost every week we'd had a nickel each to spare for ice cream. "I may go broke after school starts. How'd that garden go, anyway? Lot of work?"

"You bet your boots," said Andy, and that got us

started. We talked about the weeds and the worms, sunburn and mosquito bites and sweaty treks around town. The good stuff, too—the carrots we rinsed off with the hose and ate in the garden, the ice cream we made when we weeded Scott's garden, the ball games and all the money for stamps.

"You mean you didn't spend it all here?" Charley teased.

We had gathered an audience as more customers drifted in. A burly-looking man swiveled around on his stool at the counter. "Anybody here seen that Riggs kid lately?"

That stopped our chatter. "I think they moved," I said. "Why?"

The man turned back without answering. He drummed his dirty fingers on the counter.

"Who is he?" I whispered to Scott.

"Junker Jenkins, the junk man. Haven't you ever seen him?"

"Not up close."

The man said to Charley Sweet, "You see him, you let me know. He's got something coming to him. I want to make sure he gets it."

" 'Bout time he got what was coming to him." Andy hadn't quite come around, even after the soaker hose.

Scott and I exchanged looks.

Oh, Billy. What have you done?

CHAPTER 20

Old Wolf paced at the garden's edge, straining at the leash that kept him from romping among the Young Sprouts. I went to give him another hug. He knew something was up. "In just a little while, Wolfie," I said to him. The skinny, bedraggled creature Billy had found in the alley a few months ago was only a memory. Mr. Burt would come home to the same Old Wolf he'd left.

"He's back!" Maria whispered, and ducked her head. She kept on pulling pea pods from the tangle of vines.

"Mr. Burt!" I called as Dad's car slowed and stopped at the Burts' front walk. I ran a few steps, arms out, and then stopped. The other Sprouts froze in their places in the garden and stared. Old Wolf barked. I went back to untie him, then snapped a leash onto his collar and put my arms around his neck.

An old man, thin and hunch-shouldered, elbowed away the hands that tried to help him out of the car. Thin or not, I thought, that's Tom Burt. Still stubborn! Dad and Mrs. Burt hovered, but they waited while the man unfolded himself and positioned a wooden crutch under each arm. Mrs. Burt looked on anxiously. Dear Mrs. Burt. I wanted to run to her.

Instead I stroked Old Wolf's head and looked around at the garden. We were picking for Friday sales, so we hadn't watered. The garden had a dry summer look. I had pictured it fresh and green for the Burts' return. But Mr. Burt's eyes were on his dog.

"Here, boy," he said. I caught Old Wolf by the collar before he could bound up. He would surely knock the man down in his excitement. Holding the leash close to his head, I led him over. A smile spread into the flabby wrinkles on Mr. Burt's face. "Good dog, good dog," he said. Old Wolf nosed a crutch and growled. "It's okay, boy. It's okay."

"We'd better get you into bed, Tom Burt," Dad said, but Mr. Burt ignored him.

"Uh-oh," I heard Andy say. Instead of going up the walk to his front door, the old man turned to hobble down the walk that edged the garden. Dad and Mrs. Burt stayed close on either side, and Mother, who had hurried across the street, followed behind. Old Wolf jumped along beside them, taking me with him.

Then Burt stood, leaning on his crutches, and stared at his garden. Something in his eyes terrified me.

Tears! What did that mean?

"You. Come over here," he called. A sweep of his head said he meant everybody. The Sprouts hung back at first, then inched over.

He shot out questions. "You did this? You picked all my stuff?"

"Yes, sir." Scott was the first to find his voice. The others nodded.

"And sold it?"

"Well, yes, Mr. Burt," I said. "We thought—"

"For war bonds?"

"Yes, sir."

"Not for candy?"

I hesitated. "Mostly for bonds, Mr. Burt."

The old man made a sound I couldn't have described, somewhere between a snort and a sniffle. "Well, I'll be danged," he said. He nodded slowly as he scanned the garden.

Long minutes later, he said, "Good."

It must have taken all the energy he had, because he obeyed when Mrs. Burt and Dad began to ease him back up the walk.

I held the tomatoes under cold water and gently rubbed away the dust. Then I dried them on a dish towel and nestled them into another towel I'd stuffed into the bottom of a sack. I folded down the top of the sack and wrote T. DUEL in big letters on the side. I set it at the corner of the workroom counter, nearest the kitchen.

It was seven-thirty in the morning. The other

Sprouts wouldn't be there until eight o'clock. I filled my cereal bowl with Post Toasties and took it to the back steps. Over my shoulder, a bird sang out from the mulberry tree.

The first day of the Harvest Festival had at long last arrived. It would be hot. I felt it in the stillness of the air, but I felt excitement, too.

That day, after deliveries, and all day Saturday, we would fly from Ferris wheel to carousel, from ring toss to dart throw, and from hamburgers to hot dogs at stands along Main Street. By Saturday night we would know who had won the Great Tomato Duel. I smiled at the *Chronicle*'s exaggerated title.

Sprouts tumbled in early, eager to be finished and off to the fair. We scrambled through the garden, taking only what had to come off that day, and hurried back to the workroom with our pickings.

I had the phone order sacks lined up for them to fill, a list printed on each sack. Scott started. "Two onions," he read, and transferred them from his basket to the sack marked K. MARTIN, then moved on to the next sack. Andy came behind him, pushing him along. "Where are the women when you need them?" he complained. Neither Ellie nor Maria had shown up.

The boys piled their sacks into their bike baskets, leaving the others on the counter. Hot to get away, they tore off. The day's profits were ours for the fair.

Maria phoned just as the boys left. Her mother had been called to help a sick neighbor. It was not unusual for Maria to miss when her mother needed her, but surely Ellie would come. While I waited, I washed up and changed out of my garden clothes into a dress. I wanted to look my best when I handed the tomatoes over to the judges. Dad had already taken his, on his way to work.

I was just tying my sash when I heard the telephone ring. I dashed downstairs, knowing it would be Ellie. "My sister cut her hand, and Mama's taken her to the doctor. I need to stay with the baby," she said.

I would have to take the Sprouts' tomatoes to the judges' tent and then do the selling on our route by myself. Well, I could do that. The tomatoes weren't due until noon. I loaded the rest of the phone order sacks into the *Flying Thunder* and went back for the duel tomatoes.

At the counter I stopped short. Something was not right. My glance caught the name on the one sack left: T. BUELL. Theda Buell was on the boys' route. In their rush, they must have taken one of my sacks. In one awful instant, I understood.

Be calm, my mind said as my body thrashed around the workroom, searching. A knot twisted in my stomach. The contest tomatoes, marked T. DUEL, were in a bicycle basket, bouncing toward Theda Buell's house—if they weren't already being scalded and peeled for canning!

I hurried to the telephone, lifted the receiver, and cranked the handle to ring the operator.

"Number, please."

"Theda Buell, please," I said to the operator. I didn't have time to look up the number.

It rang until the operator came back on. "I'm sorry, Teresa, Miss Buell isn't answering."

I leaned over the slanted shelf that held the telephone notepad and laid my head on my folded arms. I could never catch up with the tomatoes. Unless—

There was a small chance that Theda Buell had missed her delivery. If she wasn't answering her telephone, perhaps she was out for the morning. The duel sack would still be with the boys, but where were the boys? They could be anywhere on their route.

If only I hadn't broken that bicycle chain! I looked at the clock. I still had time. On my skates—I sighed. My broken skates. Wait! Only one skate was actually broken. And one good skate would be faster than walking.

Seated on the front steps, Theda Buell's vegetable sack at my side, I bent to tighten my skate strap. It snapped! Could anything else happen? I buried my head in my arms.

I didn't see him so much as feel him there. "What gives?" I heard.

Billy!

I opened my eyes and looked out through my folded arms. A bicycle wheel was right by my foot.

I had never seen Billy on a bicycle. Even after he had fixed my tire, I hadn't asked if he wanted to ride. And I had never seen Billy clean! I wouldn't have recognized him if I hadn't heard his voice before I saw his ironed shirt and slicked-down hair.

But I was so stuck on my problem that I didn't tell him that he looked nice, that I had missed him, worried about him. I just blubbered out the miserable story.

"Well, geez, don't just sit there." He picked up Miss Buell's sack and slammed it into my chest, pulling me up by my arm at the same time. "Get on." His elbow pointed at the handlebars.

I shook my head and pulled at the hem of my dress. Why hadn't I left my overalls on?

He gave me a look of complete exasperation.

"I ain't got all day," he said.

What choice did I have? I bunched up my skirt to make rompers. Billy looked at the sky as I tucked the hem into the legs of my underpants.

We cut through the schoolyard and across the court-house lawn, and took alleys to avoid Main Street, where the rides and booths were still being set up. My bare legs stuck straight out in front.

"There!" All of a sudden Billy slammed on his brakes and jumped off the bicycle, leaving it and me to crash to the ground. Would I kill him or not! I was about to yell something no lady would say when I saw Billy tussling with Andy. Andy tossed the sack he thought was Miss Buell's to Scott while holding Billy off with one hand. Billy dodged and stepped sideways. His hands went up, catching the sack before Scott even saw it coming. Andy made a grab for it.

"Andy, wait!" I yelled, but his fists were already flailing.

"No!" I lit into him headfirst and knocked him off balance. If I had had time, I would have laughed. He was stunned, but he didn't dare hit a girl. "Let Billy have it, Andy. That sack is for the contest!" I said. "Those"—I pointed to the vegetables that had scattered around the bike—"are Theda Buell's."

"Come on," Billy said. He was already back on the bike, holding the duel sack out to me. We left Scott and Andy to reassemble Miss Buell's order, and raced toward the judges' tent.

We wheeled up just as the twelve o'clock whistle blew. "Made it!" we said, but at that moment someone banged a sign onto the counter: Closed. Judging in Progress.

"Just a minute! She has something!" Billy called as we hustled off the bike. He took me by the elbow and pulled me over. I set the sack on the counter, trying not to plop it down too hard, and looked up—at Theda Buell!

"We are closed," she said, thin-lipped. Her hard eyes looked over her glasses at me.

"But I—we—"

"Closed. Twelve o'clock. You heard the whistle."

I thought Billy gave up much too easily. "Come on, Teresa. You're out of luck," he said. He picked up the sack and turned to put it in the bicycle basket. As he turned he whispered to me, "Keep her talking." Then he left, bike, sack and all, leaving me standing there, flabbergasted.

Talk to Miss Buell? I had practically told her off about Scott's dad. I said the first thing that came into my head. "So this is where you've been."

"Excuse me?" She shot me a who-are-you-to-question-me look.

"I mean I—we—the boys tried to deliver your vegetables."

"I can't wait around for those rascals," she said.

"Yes, ma'am—uh, no, ma'am. I guess they were running late." Probably they had stopped off for a ride on the Loop-the-Loop. Well, that was lucky for me—almost.

She put her hands on the sign as if to emphasize her importance. I looked inside the tent, thinking of what to say next. A table along each side held baking contest entries, cakes on one, pies on the other. Stretched along the back of the tent, a third table held the tomatoes. A few were in fancy baskets. I hadn't thought of that. Most were in rolled-down paper bags. Two judges stood behind each table, looking over the entries.

"Miss Buell," I began, then stopped. Over her shoulder I saw the back side of the tent ripple. As she waited for me to go on, a very familiar paper sack rose from behind the tomato table and moved itself into place at the end of the row. My eyes widened. The tent back rippled again. Miss Buell made a half turn, as if to see what I saw, but I gripped her arm and said, "I understand, Miss Theda. Ma'am."

"You're quick," I said when I caught up with Billy.

"Gotta be," he said.

CHAPTER 21

$\mathcal{I}$ still had to go get the wagon and make the other deliveries. Billy went along, walking his bike. All at once we both seemed tongue-tied, as though we hadn't just made that crazy run with the tomatoes. He didn't mention his long absence or his new duds.

"Haven't seen you," I said.

"Been gone."

"Mm-hmm?" As if to say, where to, and why didn't you tell someone, and what about the plant?

"My grandma's."

He could have told me. "She give you the bike?"

"Nope."

We walked a while, quiet, and then he said, "My mom came back."

I hadn't known she was gone. That would explain the dirty kitchen before, and the clean shirt and combed hair now.

"From where?"

"From my grandma's. She'd been gone awhile. She had to get away. From my pop, you know. He was . . ."

"I know."

"I reckon everybody knows. But it ain't exactly like they think."

"I suppose not."

"I . . . I wasn't any angel for my mom, either. When she left to go stay with my grandma, she tried to take me. But I got out at the first filling station and walked back."

"What did your dad say?"

"He was passed out on the couch. He never knew I'd been gone. Just thought Mom had left."

"She didn't come back for you?"

"She knew I could fend for myself. I'd done it for a long time, while she was out working to put food on the table. She thought I'd call her when I got hungry enough. But I never did."

"Get hungry, or call?"

"Call. Somebody had to take care of my pop. He sure as . . . heck . . . couldn't take care of himself."

I cringed. Who did that leave to take care of Billy?

"So when did she come back?"

"Well, she came back once, right after school was out. She figured I'd go with her then, but I wouldn't leave Pop."

It seemed odd to me, a boy taking care of his father. I worried about Dad, yes. I tried to keep his mind off the danger Jeff might be in. But he and my mother took care of me. I'd always thought that's the way families were.

"So she stayed?"

"Nah, not then. But she's back again now. I went and got her."

"You—how?"

He drew a long breath, as though this would take some time.

"Well, soon after we made the soaker hose, Pop was gone for a couple of days. Really gone, not just in his head. Couldn't find him anywhere. I figured he'd gone to get Mom—get her to come home."

"What did you do?"

"I hitchhiked to my grandma's, but Pop wasn't there. Mom and I came back. Grandma too. Found Pop in a ditch, passed out, and got him to the doctor's."

"Doc Sanders? What did he say?"

"Said there wasn't nothin' he could do but send him to Topeka."

"What's there?"

"Hospital of some kind. Mom says he'll be back. Someday."

"He will." I wanted it to be true.

"About the statue," Billy said, surprising me. That seemed ages ago.

"What?"

"I did it."

"I know."

"How the hell do you know so much?" he said, not even bothering to take back his swear word.

I didn't answer, and he went right on, as if he had to get this out. "We was turnin' over an outhouse that night, them kids from junior high and me. The guy came out of his house, screamin' and yellin'. We ran off, but when he went inside we went back.

"First thing we know, the sheriff is there, sayin', 'You kids better come with me now.' The other guys got away, but I couldn't run fast enough. Sheriff put me in his car and pulled up to my house."

Billy puffed himself up and repeated what the sheriff had said. " 'I'll have a word with your father.' Huh! I said, 'Yes, sir,' and went through the kitchen and out the back door while he was waiting in the front room for my pop, who probably wasn't even there."

"Where'd you go?"

"To the Burts'. That slab the statue sits on is a good place to sleep. You can look at the stars." He stopped as though his story was finished.

"Well?"

"Well, I woke up with that wild animal's two big feet right plunk on my chest. Scared the bejeebers out o'me."

"Wolfie?"

"Exactly what I thought he was, a wolf. Didn't look anything like hisself. I sprung up and bumped into the statue. It wobbled, and I realized it wasn't stuck to the base. I pulled it down and threw it at him."

I knew the rest. "Why didn't you just tell us?"

"I couldn't have paid for the statue. And I felt awful about the dog."

"But Wolfie got well, and nobody had to pay for the statue. Dad fixed it. It's back there now."

"I know."

"Is that why you didn't come to the garden at first, because of the statue?"

"That. Looking out for Pop. Working for Junker."

"You had a job? At the junkyard? You never said."

"You never asked."

"Must have made a lot of money," I said, looking at his bike.

"Nah. A nickel a week for an ice cream, and a promise. I never figured Junker'd keep the promise." He rubbed away a smudge on his handlebars. "I mean, where can you buy a bike in wartime?"

"Junker bought the bike?"

"No. He made it, kind of. Put together old parts people had junked, somebody's frame, somebody else's tires. Junker can fix anything. It beats all. And he's a real artist with a paintbrush. Good as new!" He beamed. I couldn't get used to Billy's face being so clean.

"Something else to tell you," he said.

"What?"

"My grandma loved the tomato. Wanted to know your secret."

CHAPTER 22

I sliced a ripe tomato and laid the slices around a plate of fried chicken. In moments I was knocking at the Burts' kitchen door.

"Oh, your mother's fried chicken! Please tell her we said thank you," said Mrs. Burt.

"Sure." I hesitated, wishing I could stay for a minute.

"Come in, dear. We haven't talked in so long." I stepped in. She sniffed the chicken. "Ahh. And these tomatoes are beautiful! Now, whose are they, and who is going to win the duel this year?"

"It's hard to tell, especially since the secret weapon—" I clapped my hand over my mouth.

"You had a secret weapon? Something you used to defeat Mr. Burt the last two years?"

"Not really," I said. "I just thought we did."

I found myself telling Mrs. Burt about my foolish paintbrush idea and how I had believed it made a difference. I said I couldn't bear to mention it to Dad. "He was just pretending he believed it, too." I paused. "You and my mother were in cahoots, weren't you? You let us win so Dad would keep at his gardening and not worry so much about Jeff. Am I right?"

"Not exactly. We all wanted your dad to keep gardening, but the ladies and I really did do a blind tasting on the tomatoes. Don't you remember? You put labels on the bottom of the plates yourself and said 'Don't look until you've decided.' It just happened to come out that yours tasted better. But why do you say your idea was foolish?"

I explained what Mr. Tiller had told me. "The pollen is already there, right in the blossom. It just falls into place. The tomato pollinates itself."

"Well, it couldn't have hurt anything, and might even have helped."

"Do you think so?"

"Why don't you go ask Mr. Burt?"

Tom Burt was the last person I wanted to ask, but Mrs. Burt took me by the hand and pulled me into the living room, where her husband sat reading his newspaper. "Teresa has a question," she said.

"You figured that out all by yourself?" Mr. Burt asked me when I'd told him about the paintbrushes. "When you were just a little tyke?"

"I know it was dumb."

"Dumb, nothin'. Smart, if you ask me."

"Smart?"

"Sure. Logic told you the tomato flowers might need bees. When you decided that with the tip of a paint-brush you could do the work of the bees, well, that was just the next step in the logic."

"Except that tomatoes pollinate themselves."

"Yes, but so does corn, and some farmers hand-pollinate their corn."

"Why?"

"To get better corn." He lowered the newspaper he had been peering around as we talked. "You see, pollen falls from the tassels at the top of the cornstalk to the silks below. That makes the kernels begin to grow on the young corncobs."

"Then why . . . ?"

He folded the paper and laid it on his lap. "Suppose a farmer wants to raise a better kind of corn. He plants two kinds. Then he pollinates one kind with the pollen from the other kind, and gets corn with the best traits of both."

"But we only planted one kind of tomatoes."

"I know. But your idea of giving nature a boost wasn't so far off. Yep, pretty smart."

"See, Teresa?" Mrs. Burt said.

"Well, we did have fun believing we had the jump on you. And the brushes kept Dad and me together, and busy, after Jeff left. That took Dad's mind off the war a little bit, I think."

Mr. Burt nodded slowly, like he had in the garden.

"Maybe that's the secret," he said, and went back to his paper.

"Psst. Psst."

I turned around in my seat in the high school auditorium. Billy Riggs sat several rows back, between two women. He looked at the ceiling and then all around.

Everyone in town came to the Harvest Festival's closing ceremony. People sauntered in, some still eating cotton candy. They stopped to talk with each other and then found seats.

The Young Sprouts took up five seats in the front row. We were ready to be declared the Great Tomato Duel winner. For good luck we wore clean overalls and carried straw hats, to look like the real gardeners we had become. Except that I had my striped baseball cap.

Dad and I had eaten tomatoes from both gardens most of the summer, and we agreed we were pretty well even. To tell the truth, the tomatoes I'd seen in the judges' tent, peeking over the brims of their baskets, hadn't impressed me.

We'd have a long evening before the contest announcements would come. The high school band director lifted his baton. The noise faded to silence. The director brought the baton down, and we came to our feet, singing "The Star-Spangled Banner."

Jugglers, acrobats and a clown on a unicycle romped through acts that made the audience gasp. Little kids tap-danced, and the high school chorus sang "God Bless America." The band played the Armed Forces songs, and everyone sang, "Over hill, over dale...Anchors aweigh, my boys...Nothing can stop the Army Air Corps!"

At last the Harvest Festival chairman came to the microphone. There were people to thank and applaud. I closed it out of my mind and thought about Jeff. We had come to his commencement here, just before he enlisted.

My mind was still drifting when I heard the word *Chronicle* mentioned. The editor was being introduced to announce the Great Tomato Duel winner. I snapped to attention and crossed fingers on both hands. The editor told how the duel had started and asked Alan Marks and Tom Burt, the originators, to stand up. I turned around to see them. Mr. Burt waved from his seat, his crutches resting nearby, but Dad stood up. Mrs. Burt and Mother beamed at them. Dad looked at me and raised two fingers in a *V*-for-victory sign. Victory for whom? I would have teased him if I had been over there.

Then I was surprised to hear my own name, but it wasn't about the prizes yet. The editor repeated the story about the Young Sprouts taking over the Burts' garden. Who in town hadn't already known that? We had banged on every door. He called out our names and asked us to stand. We jumped up and waved our hats. Everybody clapped for us. That felt good!

I was still smiling and squirming in my seat when I heard, "Third prize, Mr. Alan Marks."

Third? Tears sprang to my eyes. I couldn't look back at Dad. A thousand thoughts whirred through my mind. I might have wanted to beat him, but not by that much. I should have been helping him. He had the store. I had more time, an unfair advantage.

Finally I did look back. Dad was grinning. He clasped both hands together and raised them over his head. He was rooting for me now.

"The Young Sprouts Gardeners!" A squeal stopped in my throat when I heard the rest: "Second place." I just sat there while the other Sprouts jumped up. Maria yanked at my arm, and I guess I stood up, too. The only way I had pictured second was if Dad won first.

I didn't listen for the winner. It didn't matter. How could I have been so prideful? The editor droned on, dragging it out to create suspense for the crowd.

I tried to concentrate on the good things. We had surely earned enough stamps to make our class tops in the school's war bond drive. We had saved the Burts' garden, and maybe Scott's, too. Mrs. Burt was back. Mr. Burt was doing well. He even thought I was smart! Five kids from Shady Grove Grade School had proved we could help win the war. We'd never worked so hard, but we'd had fun; that was the amazing part!

The statue mystery was solved for real, although only Billy and I knew the truth. We would probably get our platter back. Billy had shown his good side, and made me reach for mine.

A burst of applause interrupted my thoughts. The Sprouts were jumping out of their seats. Andy was pounding Scott on the back. What?

Scott's mother was making her way to the microphone. "Oh, my goodness!" she said when the editor held out the blue ribbon. She thanked him and looked out over the audience. "I thank all of you, too, for the kindness you have shown to my family during our ordeal. As you know, my husband is missing." I wondered how she could be so brave.

She continued, "I am very proud of him. He went to war for the same reason his own father went to the last war—so that his sons could grow up free." The audience thundered its applause. "One of our sons, Scott, carries a letter in his pocket. He might want to share that with you now."

I saw Scott shake his head and scoot down into his seat, but when Andy elbowed him, he got up and joined his mom at the microphone.

" 'Dear Scott,' " he read from the letter. " 'I'm a friend of Sergeant Scott Walker, your dad. We promised each other that if we ever got separated, he would write to my mom and I would write to his first son. I think you are old enough to hear this: Just before we got separated, I was on the ground with a twisted leg when an enemy grenade landed at my feet. By instinct, the troops scattered away from it, but your dad ran to pick it up and hurl it away. That saved my life. Wherever he is, your dad will know what to do. You take care of your mama, now. By the way, I hear you are quite the gardener. Your friend, Corporal Tim Jones.' "

Scott took his seat as the crowd cheered. When it quieted, Mrs. Walker said, "I'll keep the ribbon always. But this"—she held up the bond—"is for these courageous young citizens." She looked at the front row. Us? "The Young Sprouts Gardeners."

We whooped and jumped out of our seats. The whole town came to its feet, roaring. I put my hands to my face and felt wet cheeks, I don't know whether from laughing or crying.

I couldn't wait to tell Jeff.

AUTHOR'S NOTE

Your great-grandparents may have raised victory gardens like Teresa's out of patriotism or the need to put food on the table, but there was much more to it than that. Victory gardens grew forty percent—nearly half—of U.S. vegetables during the war, as Americans, in early-morning and late-afternoon hours, during lunchtime and on weekends, went to work in their backyards, front yards and vacant lots. Apartment dwellers gardened in window boxes.

Children played a big part in the effort. Those in 4-H clubs alone harvested three million bushels of vegetables and canned fourteen million jars of food. At the time, the gardeners could not have known the enormous impact their planting, hoeing and harvesting would have on the outcome of the war.

When you think about it, armies and navies, for all of their strategy, skill and courage, with their great ships, planes and guns, cannot hold out long without food. Nor can civilians who run airplane factories, shipyards and hospitals. "History proves that when nations go to war the one which fails to provide its people and its fighting men with ample food is the one that crumbles," *Life* magazine stated in 1943.

Great Britain, America's ally, knew well that in wartime, food makes all the difference. Its cities had already borne heavy bombing and its ships had endured German U-boat attacks long before the United States entered the war. Prime Minister Winston Churchill, in what he called the most important letter he ever wrote, asked U.S. President Franklin D. Roosevelt to find a way to help. That way was the Lend-Lease Act, passed by Congress, to get food, weapons and supplies to our allies. By late 1942 the United States had shipped one million tons of food to war-torn Britain. Even with Lend-Lease, their own victory gardens and food rationing, the British people suffered from hunger during the war.

Many things affected the food supply in the United States. Rationing was delayed until after shortages had already developed. Then floods ravaged Midwestern farms, just when the nation needed to provide more food than ever before in its history and faced a shortage of manpower on the farms. That shortage was addressed with the deferment of three million men from military service to create a "land army," together with government assistance to farmers, and millions of victory gardens.

Historians tell us the Allied victory in World War II saved the world. A part of that victory came because, as Teresa would say, the gardens worked.

ACKNOWLEDGMENTS

My deepest gratitude to my sister Kathi MacIver, for helping Dad with the tomatoes and for extensive manuscript critique; to our fellow writers Charlotte Huck, Mary Skillings-Prigger, Katherine Thomerson and Ruth Radlauer, for ongoing help and encouragement; to Dr. Ron Yoshino, Dr. Edward Passaro and Pat MacIver, for historical perspective; to readers Connie McNeil, Marilyn MacIver, Donna Miller, Leslie Colvin, Margaret Sharp, Helene Pendergraft and Mary Morrison, for helpful suggestions; to the Riverside Renaissance Writers and everyone at Riverside Public Library, for inspiration and support; to Françoise Bui, a most incredible editor, for patience and trust; and above all to my family, for overwhelming love and support.

ABOUT THE AUTHOR

Lee Kochenderfer grew up in small-town Kansas, where gardens were a part of life. She is a graduate of Wichita State University and holds a Ph.D. in education from the University of California, Riverside. She and her husband, Harold, live in Riverside and are the parents of three adult children. She has taught in elementary school and at Riverside Community College. Her articles and stories have appeared in newspapers and professional and literary journals. *The Victory Garden* is her first novel.

Lee invites you to visit her Web site, www.leekochenderfer.com, and welcomes your e-mails at leekochenderfer@earthlink.net.